TAILS
FROM DOWN UNDER

www.mascotbooks.com

TAILS FROM DOWN UNDER

For more information, please contact:
Mascot Books
620 Herndon Parkway, Suite 320
Herndon, VA 20170
info@mascotbooks.com

Library of Congress Control Number: 2021904955

CPSIA Code: PRV0721A
ISBN-13: 978-1-64543-785-7

Printed in the United States

Dedicated to the best siblings, Krishan and Ria.

TAILS
FROM DOWN UNDER

TARA LALA

TABLE OF CONTENTS

❦ CHAPTER 1 ❦

Ophelia's Orphanage

When you think of a morning in France, you probably imagine people sipping coffee and eating croissants in a Paris café overlooking the Eiffel Tower. You think of the birds chirping, flowers blooming, and people singing in the streets. But that's not what I wake up to. I live in an orphanage in Pauvres-Kalai, one of the dirtiest cities in France.

My morning consists of Ophelia, the orphanage owner, yelling for us to come eat our disgusting breakfast. All twenty of us girls wake up with a groan. We trod down the creaky, dusty stairs into our small eating room. Ophelia stands there, scolding us to hurry up and sit down. She says our porridge has gone cold, yet it is disgusting whether it is cold or not.

Suddenly, a mouse runs out of a hole in the wall. Ophelia shrieks, "Somebody patch up that hole!" After eating our breakfast, we do our chores while Ophelia sleeps. We make our beds, sweep the floors, and wash the windows. Ophelia doesn't feed us lunch, so we starve until dinnertime. She gives us each a piece of bread and a slice of cheese. If we are lucky, we grab seconds while she is turned away. She likes to hoard the food for herself.

After dinner, Ophelia puts on her one, plain dress and goes out into the city. She roams the streets alone, looking for someone to be her husband. She wishes every day of her life that she can get out of this dump and go live in a fancy chateau. The girls and I know she will never find a husband, for she is ugly and rude.

When Ophelia is out looking for a husband, my best friend Rosie and I sneak out. We are only seven, and we are small enough not to be seen. We hide in the shadows and take the alleys down to the ocean. The ocean isn't beautiful; its gray waters, thick fog, and trash-filled beaches don't attract many people. Although it's an ugly sight, the ocean is my favorite place to be. I've always loved it and felt a special connection to it. Rosie and I come here and sit on the shore together to watch the waves crash. After it gets dark, we rush back to the orphanage so we don't get caught by Ophelia. The other girls never rat us out, but Ophelia always catches us. We get a beating and then are sent to our room. Even though we get bruised, going to the beach will always be worth it. This is the same routine we follow every day, until one morning when we hear a knock on the front door.

We have never heard a knock on the door—nobody ever

wants to visit this orphanage. We all peer out of our bedroom door to see Ophelia opening the front door for a couple and a boy. This doesn't look like any ordinary family. Although they aren't the most beautiful people, they have glowing skin, smooth blonde hair, and bright blue eyes. They look much cleaner and fresher than all of us girls do. The maman is wearing a fancy dress with seemingly expensive jewelry. The papa and boy are wearing nice clothes and shoes. I notice the papa wearing a sparkly gold watch around his wrist. The maman looks around in disgust as she holds her boy's hand. He looks a couple years older than me. The papa forces a smile, and Ophelia quickly lets them in.

"Bonjour," Ophelia says. All of us are still upstairs, peering out from behind the door. The little boy looks up at us and frowns. We have dust all over our clothes and dirt on our faces. We don't own any of those fancy machines; we wash our clothes by hand.

"Um, hi," the papa says with an American accent. "We don't speak French."

"Ah! No worries," Ophelia replies in English, trying to act pleasant. "What brings you here?"

"We are here to adopt a child," the papa says slowly.

We look at each other in excitement. No one has ever been adopted before!

Ophelia's eyes grow wide. "Oh, of course. Well, there are plenty of girls to choose from. There is Eloise, Rosie—" She starts pointing upstairs toward us.

"Actually, we already have a little girl in mind. I think her name is Paradise," the papa says, cutting Ophelia off.

The girls quickly look at me with wide eyes.

"Paradise?" Ophelia asks in disgust. "Why would you want to adopt a little rat like her?"

The maman's eyes grow wide in horror, but I will not let Ophelia ruin my chance of leaving here forever!

I push through the girls and run down the stairs. "I am Paradise!"

"Yes, we would like to take her," the papa says.

Why would they want to take me? I wonder, but I don't ask any questions. "Hooray!" I cheer.

The maman breathes in heavily as she looks at the papa. The little boy is still staring at me with a frown.

"I cannot believe out of all the girls, they are taking Paradise," Ophelia mutters. "But at least she'll be out of my hair."

The maman's lip curls as she squeezes her husband's hand. The papa gives her a look and turns back to me. Before they can withdraw their offer, I rush up the stairs to go wash my face and make my hair look nicer.

"You're going with the rich, American family, Paradise," Krissy says.

"I know! I can't believe it!"

"Why would they want you?" Shanna asks.

"I have no idea, but it means I'm getting out of this horrible orphanage, so I don't care what their reason is for taking me. I'm free!"

"Maybe they're adopting you because you are the prettiest of all of us," says Aria.

"Your eyes are sparkling, Paradise. You must be so happy," adds the eldest girl, Eloise, as I collect my hair into a ponytail.

"Yes! Yes! I truly am." I turn to Rosie. "Rosie, do not be upset. When I go to America and become rich, I will come back and give money to all of you! Then you can be free from horrible Ophelia."

"Do you promise?" Rosie asks.

"I promise."

She smiles. I hug her and the other girls and start walking out the door until she says, "Wait! You can't forget your locket."

I quickly turn around and grab my necklace from under my bed. It is in the shape of a heart and has my name engraved in it: Paradise Royale. This is all my real parents left for me. I don't know who they were or if they are still alive today. Eloise once sent my DNA to a lab in Paris after I begged her for days. I wanted to see if I could find my parents, but there were no matches found.

I hid this locket from Ophelia because it is made of real gold. If she saw me wearing it, she would try to steal it and sell it. I decide now is the moment to wear the necklace because Ophelia won't steal it from me in front of the family, and I run out the door.

"Where did you get that locket?" Ophelia gasps as I walk toward the family.

"It is mine that I have hid from you."

"You!" she screeches. "What's inside it?"

"I don't know," I answer truthfully. "We have all tried opening it, but it will not budge."

Ophelia glares at me as I leave with the family.

"I need to get the adoption paperwork signed," says the papa after we get into their fancy car. "While I'm figuring that out, why don't you give her a bath and dress her in proper clothes when we get back to the hotel?" he asks the maman.

"You want to spend money on getting a whole wardrobe for her?" she asks.

"Yes. She is our child now, too. She can't look like this," he responds in disgust.

The maman rolls her eyes, but then agrees.

I have never been adopted before, but I was expecting a warmer welcome than this. *Why did you roll your eyes?* I want to ask my new maman. *Do you want me to be dressed in rags?*

"Where do you live?" I ask instead, trying to break up the awkwardness. I have so many questions for them.

"In Los Angeles," the boy says. He has blonde bangs covering his eyebrows.

"Where is Lost Angleez?"

"Los Angeles," he repeats. "You have a very thick French accent."

"That is because I am from France."

"Well, we need to change that," he says. "The people from

Los Angeles are cool. Like us. I'll teach you an American accent so you can fit in perfectly. And you're not that ugly. Once we freshen you up, you'll be much prettier."

"In the orphanage, I'm the prettiest girl. That's what everyone says," I say honestly.

"We'll make you even prettier when we give you new clothes," he adds. "If you're going to be my little sister, you have to be cool."

"Okay, I will be cool," I say. "How old are you?"

"Nine."

"What is your name?"

"Sam. Sam Jones," he says. "My dad's name is Paul Jones, and my mom's name is Megan Jones."

The maman and papa just sit there, silent. *Why aren't they talking to me?* I think to myself. *They were the ones who chose me out of all of the other girls in the orphanage.*

"My name is Paradise Royale," I say.

"If you were *my* child, I would have named you Jean Jones," the maman says.

I make a face because I like my fancy name. "Thank you for adopting me," I say after a moment of silence. "You do not know how horrible Ophelia and the orphanage are; Pauvres-Kalai is not a place I am happy to live in. I am so glad I can move to America and call you Maman, Papa, and Sam."

"No, no, no. It's *Mom* and *Dad,*" Sam corrects me.

"Right, yes. Thank you, Mom and Dad," I say, beaming. I have never had anyone to call Mom and Dad before, so I am very excited to use the words now.

"You're . . . um . . . welcome," Dad says. Mom doesn't respond; she just sits there in silence.

After we arrive at a beautiful hotel—which, I must say, is the grandest place I have ever seen—Mom reluctantly does my hair and gives me a pink shirt and strange pants.

"What are these pants?" I ask Sam.

"These are called jean shorts," he says. "Oh boy, I have a lot to teach you."

CHAPTER 2

LA Paradise

My best friend, Zahara, and I are sitting in our last English class of sophomore year. I am sixteen now and going to Charm High. It's a beautiful school with great teachers whom I am finally starting to appreciate.

"Good afternoon, class. Welcome to your last day of tenth grade," my teacher, Ms. Art, says. "To conclude the semester, you all will be writing an essay on transformation. It will be about your growth this year. You have the whole class to finish it. Good luck."

Zahara and I look at each other, smiling. We know we're about to rock this essay. We weren't always like this, though. Three months ago, we were slacking students and only cared about popularity and looks.

THREE MONTHS EARLIER, MARCH

Sam fully Americanized me. With his guidance, I had become the most beautiful and most popular girl at Charm High, and I had no trace of French left in me. I hadn't spoken the language since I left Ophelia's Orphanage. Although I could still understand French, I could barely speak it anymore. I was a true Los Angeles girl. Zahara and I became best friends last year in ninth grade, and we'd been the queen bees of the school ever since. We wanted to grow up and become world-renowned models, so we couldn't care less about school. We were nearly failing almost every class, and every teacher hated us. Zahara's older sister, Jayla, kept telling us to pay attention in school. She was working to earn a medical degree and did not support our dreams of becoming models.

Jayla wasn't the only one who didn't support me; my parents didn't, either. Mom and Dad had always been against my dreams. Even though I was so appreciative that they adopted me, they seemed not to care about me; they only doted on Sam. Although Sam was spoiled and got whatever he wanted, he'd grown to be a humble and nice guy. Sam was now a senior and wanted to become a movie director. Mom and Dad fully supported him, but whenever I brought up modeling, they immediately criticized my dream. Sam was the only Jones who showed love toward me. He always had my back and had treated me like a little sister from the moment we left Pauvres-Kalai.

Since my parents showed no real love for me, I turned to popularity to fill that emptiness inside of me. People at school loved me. They wanted to be me; they were obsessed with me! Zahara and I loved the attention, and that is what we were devoted to . . . not studying. On the last day before spring break, we had Ms. Art's English class. Zahara and I came in late, as usual. Ms. Art rolled her eyes and told us to take a seat quickly.

"Hello, class. As you all know, this is your last class before spring break. So, I decided to give you a fun project. Today we are going to do a creative writing assignment!" Half of the class groaned, including me and Zahara. "I want you to write an essay about what you're going to be doing over spring break. Have fun!"

"Ugh," I whispered. "I don't want to do this assignment. What are you going to write about?"

"Jayla surprised us and booked my family a trip to New York," Zahara whispered back. "So, I'm going to write about that. I'm assuming you're going to write about how you're traveling to Italy?"

"Yeah."

"Paradise. Zahara. No talking!" Ms. Art called out.

We sighed and began writing.

Paradise Royale
Ms. Art
March 21, 2022

Spring Break Essay

This spring break, I'm traveling to the Amalfi Coast in Italy with my family. I'm pretty excited TBH. I'm gonna go shopping, swimming, and take tons of pics for Instagram. I'm going with my parents and my senior brother, Sam.

When I'm there, I'm gonna go to the island of Capri, which I am most excited about. I looked it up online, and it's sooo beautiful and has a lot of shops. And gelato! I honestly feel bad for using my dad's credit card, but it's okay. He's the one who chose to adopt me . . . right? Is it okay to feel that way? I don't want to disrespect them. They were the ones who took me away from the horrible orphanage.

My goal for when I am there is to be noticed by famous designers. I really want to be a model when I grow up. My best friend, Zahara, thinks I should be. She says my long brown hair, sparkling brown eyes, and tall, model-like body should be able to get me there.

I am so excited for spring break and to get away from this filth of a school!

"Time's up!" Ms. Art announced. "Hand your essays in. I'll grade them right now."

Right now?

"Why can't she just grade them when we're on break?" I whispered to Zahara as Ms. Art collected our papers. I quickly took out my mini-mirror to make sure the stress of writing that essay didn't make me sweat. Once I realized that my makeup was still perfect, I said, "I don't need to leave this place knowing I got another—"

"F!" Ms. Art yelled. Her voice echoed in the classroom. "Paradise Royale, are you out of your mind?"

"There's no way you've already finished reading my whole essay," I said.

"Whole essay? Paradise, there was barely anything to read!" Ms. Art was shaking her head dramatically.

"Please, Ms. Art. I really don't want to leave here with negative vibes," I told her.

"Negative vibes?" Ms. Art screeched. "Negative vibes?! Paradise, I am so fed up with you and your lack of interest! I want you to really think about how you've been doing in my class this year. When you come back from break, I expect a change in behavior. I know you can do better than this! Being popular is not important. Passing school is! If you just tried . . ." Her passionate voice trailed off.

I narrowed my eyes but didn't say anything. Ms. Art just sighed and went back to grading. What a way to end the last day before spring break. What a way.

"How was school, Sam?" Mom asked as we were driving home.

"It was good. We started planning our senior prank," Sam said, whipping his hair.

"How fun!" Mom added. "Paradise? Did you get yourself into any trouble?"

I rolled my eyes. She never asked if I had a nice day. "Nah. Not as bad as usual," I mumbled.

"What was that?" she asked. Suddenly, her phone started ringing. "Who's this? Another private caller?"

Sam looked at me and winked. Thank goodness. He saved me from getting into even more trouble.

"Ugh, all these children trying to prank call," Mom said, annoyed. "So rude! Anyways, what were we talking about?"

"Our trip," Sam said. "How we need to leave the house by six o'clock tonight."

"Oh, that's right." She was honestly a bit dim-witted. "Yes. Be ready by six."

We pulled up to the house, and I hopped right out. I said hi to my dad, who looked as though he had just gotten back from work and was sipping coffee at the kitchen table. When I got upstairs, I started packing my second suitcase. One was for the usual: fashionable clothes, toiletries, and shoes. My other suitcase was filled with oils, creams, face and hair masks, and most importantly, makeup. Especially

Fenty Beauty, my absolute favorite makeup brand. I insisted on looking fabulous; this was my big chance to become a world-renowned model! I packed my most expensive jewelry, dresses, and makeup. Now, I could only hope for the best.

"Sam, sweetie. Paradise. Come downstairs!" Mom called out.

It was only four o'clock. I groaned and went downstairs. My parents were sitting in our lounge area. Not to be rude, but everyone in my family was pretty plain-looking. They were not ugly, but they were not outstandingly pretty, either. That's where everyone gets confused on how I fit in to this family. I was the polar opposite. When I went to Italy, everyone would see what kind of model they were missing out on. *I am gorgeous!*

"We called you two down here because we have a surprise." Mom grinned, showing her teeth.

"Oh yeah?" I asked. Usually, their surprises were pretty lame when it came to me. For example, five years ago:

"Sam, Paradise, we have a surprise for you!" Mom called.

"Coming, Mom!" I replied. I was still cherishing having someone to call Mom.

Sam and I raced down the stairs.

"What? What is it?" Sam asked.

"Paradise, we got you a $4 gift-card to the Milkshake Palace!" Dad exclaimed.

"Really?" I beamed. I had never gotten a surprise before. "Sam gets one too, right? I don't want him to feel left out!"

"Oh, no. Sam doesn't get a card to anywhere," Dad said. "He gets a puppy!"

Mom ran back in the door with a new puppy in her hands. So, like I said, surprises were never great for me. I really didn't understand why they adopted me if they were going to treat me so much worse than Sam.

No. I needed to snap out of it.

I was lucky that I even got adopted in the first place. Sometimes, I needed to remind myself of that.

"Well? What's the surprise?" Sam asked now.

"We ordered a limousine to take us to the airport!" Mom squealed.

Wait. A limo? As in, the cars the stars take? This was a perfect way to attract attention. I could make myself look famous at one of the busiest airports in the world. Score!

"Best surprise ever," I said. And I actually meant it.

"That *is* pretty cool," Sam added.

"Good. I was hoping you'd like it," Dad said. "Well, go relax. We leave in a couple of hours."

Relax? Very funny. It was time for me to style myself!

CHAPTER 3

Airport Chic

I walked out of the house in a pink shirt, white jeans, the golden locket with my name on it, and tennis shoes. I was going to wear heels, but my parents insisted that I wear sneakers. I put on my large celebrity sunglasses and carried the fanciest purse I owned. You should look stylish everywhere you go. Once I got into the limousine, I took a glass and poured myself some cider, which was one of the luxuries that came with the car. I was going to leave America with my name as a signature, and come back with it as an autograph.

"We're here," Dad said after the forty-five-minute drive.

It's time, I said to myself.

We put all of our suitcases in a trolley for my dad to push. It was time for me to strut like I was Kendall Jenner on the runway. I put my glasses on, hung my purse around my arm, and started walking. I held my head up and walked ahead of my parents. I could not have them embarrassing me.

As I was walking, there were people of all ages looking at me . . . but surprisingly, not all in the best way. A mom looked me over from head to toe, shook her head in disgust, and walked away. Her young quadruplet sons, on the other hand, couldn't stop staring at my beauty. As I walked inside, a taller woman caught my eye. *Wait . . . that couldn't be–?*

"Rihanna!" A bunch of fan girls squealed. They were running up to her with their phones out for selfies.

But she wasn't interested in them at all. She had her eye on something else—someone else . . . me.

OH MY GOSH! Rihanna was looking at me! Did she think I was famous? Or, better yet, was she thinking of asking me to model for her makeup line, Fenty Beauty?!

She tipped her glasses down to give me another look, then put them back on. It looked like she had a slight frown, but she couldn't have . . . right? No one ever frowned when looking at Paradise Royale. She turned and started walking away with her bodyguard.

"Wait! Ri—" I started. Suddenly, I felt a tap on my shoulder.

"*Your Highness?*" a woman with a big hat and even bigger sunglasses than mine asked with a puzzled look.

"Huh?" I said and took off my glasses.

"Oh! I'm so sorry, you looked like—"

"Guys, it's Sheila Meela!" yelled one of the girls who'd been following Rihanna. She was pointing at the woman who had just approached me.

Wait a second. I was talking to *the* Sheila Meela. As in, the woman crowned most beautiful mixed girl in the world and the most famous model of *Vogue*?

The girls who'd been following Rihanna started chasing after Sheila. She gave me one last look and disappeared into the crowd with her bodyguard.

"Paradise!" my mom suddenly called from behind me. "You can't just wander off like that!"

"I just saw Rihanna and Sheila Meela," I said, feeling dazed.

"Okay, Paradise. Let's go," Dad added. My dad and Sam couldn't care less about celebrities, but my mom was obsessed.

"Wait!" Mom said as we were walking. "You saw *the* Rihanna? As in, the famous singer? *And* Sheila Meela?"

"I saw *the* Rihanna and *the* Sheila Meela," I repeated. "If I could just have a chance to have a conversation with them . . . they could make me a world-famous model. My dreams could all come true!"

"Now, Paradise, we told you. You're not allowed to become a model," Mom said. "You're just not pretty enough. And as a mom, I tell you that from the bottom of my heart because I love you."

Obviously, she just wanted to crush my dreams, but I knew that if I did become a world-famous model, she would make sure everybody knew she was my mom.

"But I would make a great model," I groaned.

"I think you should let Paradise be whatever she wants to be," Sam said. "After all, I want to work in the movie industry."

"Do whatever you want to do, Sammy-boo," Mom said.

I rolled my eyes as we walked through security. I just didn't understand why they babied him so much. As I walked through the security buzzer, it began to beep.

"Ma'am, we're going to need to check you with our scanner. Is that alright?" the security lady asked.

"Um, okay, but I definitely do not have anything on me—"

"Please stand still," the lady said firmly. As she was passing over my body, the scanner beeped right when it got to my necklace. "We'll have to confiscate this. Take it off."

"What? But I've never taken it off. Not since I left France . . ."

"Give." She motioned with her hand. "Or else there might be some serious consequences."

So rude. I took off my necklace and gave it to her. I really was attached to it. If anything happened to it, I would sue LAX Airport!

"We'll bring this back to you after we take a look at it. What is your name and airline that you are flying?"

"Paradise Royale," I said. "I'm flying Air Ria Airlines to Sorrento, Italy."

"Okay. We'll return this as soon as possible."

"What exactly are you going to do with my locket?"

"We need to open it up and make sure nothing is inside of

it. I already tried opening it, but since it won't budge, we'll need to open it with a tool."

"It's impossible, trust me. I've tried opening it, too."

The security lady looked at me suspiciously. "We will open the locket and make sure nothing harmful is in there."

I rolled my eyes. *They'd better not ruin my necklace.* "Good luck with that."

After the security drama, we waited around for about forty-five minutes and then finally boarded the plane. Since we were flying in business class, the seats were positioned like little pods: two together with the seats facing one another. Somehow, Dad messed up the ticket arrangements so we all ended up sitting across from strangers. Great. I wasn't in the mood to sit across from a random person for the next twelve hours. Plus, that meant I couldn't relax. I had to put on my famous face.

"No cameras, please," I suddenly heard someone say from the front of the plane. *Rihanna? Rihanna was on my flight!*

She briskly walked toward me, but before she got to my pod, she sat down across from my mom. This day couldn't have gotten any better. Actually, it could have, if she were sitting across from me . . . but still.

"Hiii." My mom grinned wide and shook Rihanna's hand. "I'm Megan."

Rihanna gave an awkward nod and got settled into her seat. When I looked back over to the seat across from me, it wasn't empty anymore. I couldn't believe my eyes. I was sitting across from Sheila Meela. I didn't even notice her come and sit in her seat. How did I get so lucky to be on a flight with two world-famous celebrities?

"Oh! Hello again," Sheila said. She had an interesting accent. It wasn't American, but it wasn't Italian, either. "I never properly introduced myself. Since we're sitting across from each other for the next twelve hours, might as well get to know each other. I'm Sheila."

"I know," I said, stunned she was talking to me. "I'm Paradise."

"Paradise," she repeated with a pondering look. Suddenly, her phone rang. "Eh, if you will excuse me."

As the flight took off, Mom and Rihanna struck up a conversation.

"So, you're a mom. Very nice," Rihanna said. "How many children do you have?"

"Well, that's my son, Sam," Mom explained, pointing over at Sam who was in the middle of watching a movie. "He wants to work in the movie industry one day."

"Wow, that's cool. It's a fun industry," Rihanna added. There was a pause. *Really, Mom?*

I got up out of my seat and walked to my mom. "Hey, Mom, do you have my fashion magazine?"

"Your what?"

"Oh, and you have a daughter?" Rihanna asked, looking back and forth, trying to see the resemblance.

"Oh, well, we adopted her," Mom said. "Her name is

Paradise."

"Paradise," she said. "I saw you in the airport. At least, I think that was you."

"It was," I replied sweetly.

"And what do you want to be when you grow up? In the movie industry, too?" Rihanna asked.

"Actually, I want to be a—"

"Found it! It was at the very bottom of my bag. Next time, just keep your magazines in your own bag," Mom said. *She just ruined my chance!* "Oh, and sorry to cut you off, Rihanna. She wants to do nothing with the movie, music, or modeling industry."

Arghhh! "I said I wanted to be a—"

Suddenly the plane started shaking. "All passengers," a voice over the intercom announced, "please take your seats. There is going to be turbulence for the next few minutes."

I shot my mother an evil look and headed back to my seat. At least I still had a chance with Sheila.

"So, you work as a world-top model?" I asked her.

"I do . . . oh, and that's the latest *Vogue* that I'm featured in." She chuckled awkwardly as I held the magazine with her face on the front page. Her light-brown skin was glowing and her pearly white teeth shined as she showed off her short, curly blonde hair and bright green eyes.

"Yes . . . " I trailed off, imagining myself on the front page of a *Vogue* magazine. "I think you are such an inspiration. I want to be a model when I grow up."

"Really?" she said, stroking her golden hair. "I'm glad I can be an inspiration for teenagers like you! I really wish you the best of luck. You truly are a very pretty girl."

"Thank you! Any suggestions on how you think I should start up my career?"

"Plenty. But for now, I will sleep. I haven't slept in twenty-four hours because it was my last day of shooting for another cover. I am just so glad to finally be going home." She yawned and immediately fell asleep.

A few hours later, I was in a deep sleep, too. Unfortunately, no one got the cue that I was exhausted.

"Ah, ciao, bella!" I heard someone say loudly beside me. I didn't understand Italian, but if she was talking to me, I knew she just called me beautiful.

"Um, hi," I said groggily.

"I finally found time to bring you your necklace." The flight attendant handed me my locket. "I was just so busy before! The airport wanted to give their apologies for the, um . . . "

"They scratched my locket!" I screeched. The "e" at the end of Royale was scratched out. Now, it just said Paradise Royal.

"They are really, very sorry," the flight attendant said sadly. "They confiscated it because it triggered the scanning device. They got suspicious because no matter how hard they tried, they couldn't open the locket! But eventually they realized it was just heavy gold."

"Great." They ruined the only thing my real parents left for me. The flight attendant nodded and shuffled away. She was so loud, I was surprised Sheila didn't wake up. She really must've been exhausted.

"Ciao!" the flight attendant boomed and woke me up again. "Would you ladies like anything for breakfast?"

"What do you have?" I asked sleepily.

"Toast, cereal, and a delicious seafood platter."

"Bleh!" Sheila exclaimed loudly. The flight attendant looked stunned. "Sorry, I just really do not like seafood. I think it's so rude to be eating poor, innocent animals!"

"Yeah, I've never liked seafood, either," I added.

"Oh, that's alright," the flight attendant said a little awkwardly.

"I'll have toast," Sheila said.

"And I'll have cereal."

"Okay, thank you," the flight attendant replied and scurried off.

"She is so loud," Sheila complained. "I was in the middle of a great dream!"

"I know," I said, rubbing my eyes.

"That's a very beautiful necklace," Sheila said, examining my locket.

"Thanks. The airport scratched it all up, though."

"Paradise, where did you get it?" Sheila asked curiously.

"My parents . . . well, my real parents," I said. "It's the only thing they left for me."

"Interesting . . ." Her voice trailed off. "Have you ever had any interest in finding your parents?"

"Yes, and believe me, I've tried. Nothing has been found." After living for a few years in America, my parents allowed me to send in another DNA test to find my real parents. Mom seemed a little too excited. Still, no results were found. "Watch them be some magical creatures or something," I joked.

"Paradise," Sheila looked me dead in the eye and grabbed my wrist. "There are a lot of magical creatures out in the world. Believe me, they are real. If you just believe, you will find them. Don't take fantasy or magic as a joke. Look beyond. Look deeper."

Okay, I was getting creeped out. Did Sheila Meela just turn wacko on me or what?

"Um," I started. But no other words came out.

"*Deeper,*" she repeated, still staring at me. I swore she hadn't blinked, and she was still holding onto my wrist.

I immediately got up and walked over to my mom. She and Rihanna weren't talking anymore. Rihanna had put up her privacy divider. "Can we switch seats?"

"What?" Mom asked.

"Sheila is creeping me out. Can we switch?" I begged.

"No, Paradise. Rihanna and I are really hitting it off!"

I rolled my eyes and walked back to my seat.

"Sorry if I freaked you out, Paradise," Sheila said. "You just have a very . . . magical aura."

"Okay . . . I think I'm going to go back to sleep," I said and shut my eyes. I ignored her for the remainder of the flight. Forget getting tips from this girl. I'd have to figure something else out.

After we landed and got our bags many hours later, we headed over to the shuttle taking us to the Sirena Mare Hotel. The seats were in threes, so, of course, I got booted out from sitting with my family. But it was fine! At least I was on the coast of Italy, right? When I walked over to the only open seat, Sheila the-freak Meela was there.

"Sheila?" I asked. "Shouldn't you be taking a car home?"

"No. I decided I need a vacation from my vacation," Sheila said.

"What?"

"And I've decided I want to help you find your parents," she added proudly.

"*What?*" I asked. I mean, if she weren't a weirdo, this would've been the coolest thing ever. But she was, so I didn't know how to feel!

"I think we just may be able to find your parents here—in Italy!" she exclaimed.

Why would she think that? I took my phone out to text my bestie.

Me: Zahara, I need to talk to you!

Zahara: Paradise! Hey girl! What's up?

Me: You won't believe who I met on the plane . . .

CHAPTER 4 🐚

The Sirena Mare

I love the ocean. I'm always in my happiest state whenever I go to the beach. Italy is full of beautiful cities, but I was so happy my family chose to go to the Amalfi Coast. The small, cobblestone streets were buzzing with tiny cars; I wasn't even sure how our shuttle was fitting through the streets. There were tons of boats and yachts by the shore, and the hills were glimmering with the lights of small Italian shops. It was like a painting.

"Beautiful, isn't it?" Sheila sighed.

"Yeah, I feel like I just fell into a picture."

"Signore e signori, siamo arrivati al L'hotel Sirena Mare," the shuttle driver said.

"We don't speak Italian!" one guy yelled.

Sheila stood up. "He is saying we have arrived at the Sirena Mare Hotel."

"Sheila Meela?" the guy said. Everyone turned around.

She immediately sat down.

"Sometimes I forget I am famous," Sheila whispered to me.

When we got out of the shuttle, Sheila approached my parents.

"Ah, hello! You must be Paradise's parents," she asked.

"Yes!" my mom said. Oh, so *now* she was proud because a celebrity started talking to her about me.

"She is such a sweetie! We formed a great friendship over the flight. I was wondering, may I join you all for dinner tonight?" she asked.

"Of course!" Mom answered, delighted.

"We're going to dinner right now at the hotel's restaurant," Dad added.

"Fantastic! I will be there shortly," Sheila said and walked into the lobby.

"Why did you let her come? She's psycho!" I said.

"Paradise, you're the one who wants to be a model. Embrace this," Sam said. I groaned and started walking to the restaurant.

The restaurant was under a rose-covered trellis overlooking the ocean. The sun was setting, and the sky was turning orange and pink. The piano player started playing soft and soothing songs, and there was a light breeze in the air. I was in heaven. Zahara really would have enjoyed this. I told her about the plane ride here, and she thought Sheila was crazy now, too. She was totally jealous I saw Rihanna, though.

Tonight, she was leaving for New York and hoping she'd see a celebrity in the airport.

As I looked out over the horizon, I thought of Rosie from the orphanage. We used to watch the sunsets together in Pauvres-Kalai. We used to dream about going on vacations like this—sparkling turquoise waters, white-sand beaches, and clear skies. I felt a pang of sadness inside me. Where was Rosie now? Was she still suffering at Ophelia's Orphanage? Was she able to escape and lead a better life? I probably would never know. I never tried sending letters because Ophelia would never allow us to read any of the mail that came through. She never liked me or Rosie, and I knew she wouldn't want me to make Rosie happy by sending her letters; Ophelia was selfish in that way. She only wanted herself to be happy.

"This is so relaxing," Sam said, leaning back in his chair.

"I'm exhausted," Dad said. "Let's make this a quick dinner and go straight to sleep."

"But *Sheila Meela* is coming to dinner with us!" Mom pleaded.

"Hello," Sheila suddenly came into the restaurant and pulled up a chair. She had a new bodyguard at her side and saw us all staring at him. "Oh, don't mind him. He's just going to make sure no crazy fans try to take pictures of us."

"Um, he doesn't look like your bodyguard from earlier," I said.

"He's not the same one from before," Sheila replied. "I

have one in America, one here, and one in . . . never mind."

"Where?" Mom asked nosily.

"Um . . . er . . . Australia!"

"Oh, how cool! Australia must be beautiful," Dad mused.

"Yes, very," Sheila said. "So, what are your plans for tomorrow?"

"We are going to the island of Capri for shopping!" I exclaimed. I love shopping.

"Capri is such a beautiful island!" Sheila added. "You must go to the Blue Grotto."

"What's that?" I asked.

"It's a cave. You take a small gondola into the entrance. Inside is a huge pool of ocean water, but it's the bluest ocean water you will ever see. It *glows*. The best part is that it's all natural!"

"It sounds beautiful, but we can't do it," Dad said. "The website for buying tickets to the Blue Grotto said it's closed tomorrow."

"Oh . . . that's tomorrow?" Sheila pondered. Then, a small smile spread across her face. "Um, Mr. and Mrs. . . . . Actually, I never asked your names. How rude of me!"

"Oh, no problem, sweetheart! You don't need to call us Mr. and Mrs. Jones. I'm Megan, and my husband's name is Paul."

"*Sweetheart?*" Sam asked in disgust. "Mom . . ."

"It's all right," Sheila said. "I'm twenty. So, I assume I'm a good twenty years younger than them."

"You're right," Mom said.

"Okay, cool," Sheila said. "Anyways, Paul and Megan, I was wondering, can I take Paradise to the Blue Grotto? I have a few connections . . . and being a top model with quite a bit of money always helps. I think Paradise will love it."

What? Why would she pay so much for me to go? We barely knew each other.

"Can we all go?" Mom asked.

"Unfortunately, asking a favor for more than two people is asking for too much. I am so sorry."

"I guess she can go with you," Dad said.

"I guess." Mom clenched her teeth.

"Relax, Mom. She'll be fine," Sam said.

"Excellent!" Sheila cut in as if she wouldn't take no for an answer. "So, we will meet in the lobby tomorrow morning at ten o'clock. Ah, look, the waiter is here!"

The next morning, I woke up to a loud ringing. I was hoping to just wake up with the Italian sun on my face, but obviously that didn't happen.

"You want me to tell Paradise?" I heard my Mom say from outside my room. We were staying in a suite, and my room was closest to the lounge area, so I could hear my mom talking loud and clear. "Of course, Sheila, anything for you.

Get well soon!"

I walked out of my room sleepily. "I heard my name."

"Sheila's sick. She said she thinks she caught the flu. She just won't stop throwing up! But she said she left you a driver and . . . a private yacht." My mom gritted her teeth.

"She left all that just for me?" I asked, stunned. "Well, don't mind if I do. I need to get used to this lifestyle."

Mom just stared at me in envy as I walked back into my room. It was time to dress up and get ready to get people's attention. *Luxurious model life, here I come!*

CHAPTER 5

From Tales to Tails

When Mom, Dad, Sam, and I walked out of the lobby, a driver with a fancy white car was waiting. He walked over and opened the door for me. I could tell Mom was annoyed, but she tried not to show it. They got into their taxi and waved bye to me. Dad made me promise to meet them back at the hotel by seven o'clock to get ready for dinner. My driver said the captain of my yacht was a good friend of his and that he was never late. After I stepped into the car, I rolled down my window and put on my sunglasses. It was showtime.

The temperature was blazing hot, so I made sure to bring my bikini top and swimming shorts to take a dip in the ocean. Plus, swimming actually gives you a good tan. As we drove through the busy streets, a lot of people were looking at me and poking each other. They totally thought I was famous: fancy white car, driver, and a beautiful Paradise. I waved to some people who took out their phones to take a picture of me. When we got to the dock, there were tons of boats and yachts. The captain came out, greeted me, and then took my bags. I noticed a lot of tourists staring.

A little girl ran up to me. "Are you famous?"

"Yes," I lied.

"Mom! Dad! She is famous!" The girl screamed with joy. "Can I take a picture with you?"

"Okay, but only one. I have a yacht to catch." I grinned. Her parents took a picture then thanked me, and I walked away very happy. The yacht had an indoor lounge, two bedrooms, a bathroom, and an outdoor sitting area in the front of the yacht just for me. Wow!

"Where to first?" the captain asked.

"The Blue Grotto."

As the yacht started pulling away into the ocean, I made my way to the front to relax and sunbathe. As the yacht started picking up its pace, the sea water started spraying in my face and hair. There went the perfect hair and makeup. After about thirty minutes, we arrived at the beautiful island of Capri. Its lush greenery and turquoise waters were like a dream. There were plenty of boats all around the island, but as we started pulling up to the entrance of the Blue Grotto, there was only one tiny boat with a man standing in it. The small boat was floating next to a small hole in the mountainside, which seemed to be the entrance to the Grotto.

"Ciao!" my captain called, pulling up next to the tiny boat.

"We are here for the Blue Grotto."

"Ah, welcome!" The man's face brightened up. "I hope you enjoy."

The man took off the rope blocking the entrance of the cave.

"I'm going to jump in and swim into the Grotto," I told my captain. It was obvious the yacht couldn't fit through the small hole leading into the cave. "Can you meet me at the dock at 5:15? I'll swim back to shore. It doesn't seem too far. I want to swim in here for a little and then go shopping."

"Of course! Instead of swimming to shore, those steps can lead you to the shops on the island," my captain said. He pointed to a square ledge about thirty feet away from the entrance of the cave. There were stairs on the ledge leading up to the top of the mountain. "Once you reach the top of the stairs, the road will lead you directly to the shops. The dock is near the beach, so you can ask a taxi driver to take you there when you are finished. See you soon, ma'am."

I jumped off of the yacht and swam through the small entrance. *Woah.* Inside, the cave walls were dark and black, but the water was just as Sheila said. It was the bluest water I had ever seen, and it was glowing. It was a big, circular pool, and I was surprised how this beautiful wonder was hidden in an island in the middle of the Tyrrhenian Sea. I wondered how deep the pool went.

I started swimming down—deeper and deeper. I never reached the bottom. I quickly swam back up. This pool was very deep, but I was determined to get to the bottom of it. I'm actually able to hold my breath for a long time. I've never counted for how many minutes, but it's a really strange talent. My parents once thought I drowned in the ocean because I was under the surface for so long. I couldn't help it, though. The ocean really fascinates me. Rosie and I even used to have competitions in the ocean to see who could hold their breath longer. I always won.

I took a deep breath and started swimming deeper and deeper. I'm a fast swimmer, so if it took you two minutes to swim from one side of a pool to the other, it would only take me thirty seconds. I was also lucky in that salt water doesn't bother my eyes, so swimming in the ocean has never been a problem for me.

After what seemed like a long time, I finally reached the bottom. I looked up, and woah, I was really far down. I started looking around because I wasn't desperate for air yet. Since the cave water glowed, it was easy to see. I noticed that there was something strange about the bottom of this grotto. The sand was normal, but the cave wall was different from how it was at the top of the water. There was a huge rock that looked like it was blocking a hole . . . or maybe even an entrance; and there was a crystal nestled above it.

I swam over and tried to move the boulder, but it wouldn't budge. I kicked myself upward and tried to grab the crystal. It was stuck in the wall. As I let go of the crystal, my necklace started to gravitate toward it. And then it stopped.

I looked down and saw that the letters of my name were glowing. When I looked back up, I noticed the crystal was glowing, too. My locket suddenly popped open and shot out a ray of light toward the crystal. *What on earth is happening?!* I thought.

I pulled the necklace over my head so I could look at my finally opened locket. Suddenly, the huge rock started descending into the ground. *Woah.* With the boulder buried three quarters of the way in the sand, a hole opened up that was big enough for me to swim through. I put my heavy locket into the pocket of my swimming shorts and swam through the archway . . . into the middle of the open ocean. *How is this even possible?* I thought to myself. *I was just in a cave in the middle of an island, and now I'm in the middle of the ocean?* Suddenly, a current moved me. My shorts felt lighter.

"Oh. My. Mermaid. *Human!*" I heard a high-pitched voice scream from behind me. I must've been hallucinating. People can't speak under water . . .

I turned around. In front of me were two identical young mermaids. *Mermaids!*

I started feeling dizzy. I didn't know whether it was because I just saw mermaids or because I was running out of oxygen. Maybe both.

"Breathe!" One of the mermaids said. "You can breathe!"

What?! I mean, I had no other choice, so I took a chance and released a big breath. And then I inhaled.

"Ahhh!" I screamed. "I'm breathing underwater! I'm

talking underwater! Who are you?"

The two mermaid girls looked at each other. "We're from the Reef family."

There was a pause. "Uhh, aren't you going to tell me your names?"

"I'm Millie," said the calmer-looking mermaid skeptically.

"And I'm Queenie," said the more worried-looking one. "How did you even get here?"

"I . . . I . . ." I was at a loss for words.

"We need to take you to the royal family," Millie said. "Follow us."

They started swimming away, and I followed behind their dirty-blonde hair.

"What are we going to do?" I heard Queenie whisper. "This hasn't happened since The Accident."

"Shhh!" Millie said. "We cannot disclose any information. We don't know who she is or how she got in!"

"What family did you say you were from?" Queenie asked.

"Huh? You mean, what's my last name? But shouldn't you be asking for my first name . . . "

"No. Here in Aquaria, we first introduce ourselves by saying what family we are from," Queenie said.

"Okay, well, I'm from the Roy . . ."

"Wait!" Queenie exclaimed. "I forgot to tell you about our law. Each merfolk must introduce themselves with the current family they are in. For example, if you get married, you introduce yourself by your married name."

"Well, that's not much different from where I come from," I said. "I am from the Jones family."

"And what's your first name?" Millie asked.

"Paradise."

"Paradise Jones, interesting," Millie pondered. "Let's swim faster. We need to get you to the royal family before the daily news reaches them first."

"Wait, how exactly did you know that I would be able to breathe underwater?"

"Well, it's impossible for ordinary humans to hold their breath for as long as you held it. When we realized you held it coming all the way down the Blue Grotto and through the entrance, we figured that there must be something special about you," Millie explained.

"Interesting."

They started swimming faster, so I did, too.

"We need to take a detour; we can't let any merfolk see her," Queenie said to her twin sister. "Should we take her through the secret entrance?"

Millie sighed. "I guess it's our only choice."

We were swimming through what seemed like the countryside of Aquaria, and I felt a strange tingle throughout my body. There were a bunch of coral reefs and seaweed beds. We made our way through what looked like a big, glistening city, and saw an enormous statue of a family in the middle of the town. The mermaid and mermen statues were wearing fancy jewelry and were positioned in a rather regal way. The merman was holding a large scepter. The mermaid next to him had her hand placed on another mermaid's shoulder, who was holding a baby merman, and another mermaid was holding a tiny mermaid's hand. There were six of them all together.

Around the statue, there were several colorful shops with mermaids and mermen swimming all around. There were cafés, boutiques, restaurants, and more. In the far distance, there appeared to be what had to have been a palace. It was made out of crystal. On both ends of the statue, there were two see-through hoops, like large circus rings. Next to each hoop lay a keypad. There was a line of mermaids and mermen at each, and the mermaid in the front of one of the lines punched something into the keypad. The hoop started scanning her, and when it stopped, she swam through it and disappeared.

"Woah! How did she do that?" I asked Millie and Queenie.

"Those are portals. They lead you into your neighborhood. You punch in your address, the circle scans you to make sure you aren't an intruder, and then it lets you into the portal to your neighborhood," Millie explained.

"Yeah, after The Accident, they had to have our homes hidden somewhere safe," Queenie said. Millie shot her a look. "Oops."

"The Accident? What's that?" I asked.

"We aren't the mermaids to tell you," Millie said, then something behind me seemed to catch her eye. "Oh no, the

Gossiping Goosefish. Quick, follow me!"

Millie and Queenie quickly swam and hid me behind some coral. "The Gossiping Goosefish?" I asked as a large, brown fish swam by.

"Yes, the Gossiping Goosefish," Queenie repeated. "She lives for the drama. She used to be bullied because of how ugly she was when she was little. The only reason merfolk liked her was because she told them all the gossip going on. Now, she works for *The Narwhal Newspaper*. I mean, of course she likes to gossip—have you seen the size of her mouth? But we can't let her see you. The merfolk will freak out!"

"That's why we're taking the secret sand passages to the palace," Millie said. We swam to a dead seaweed plant. Millie and Queenie pulled on it with all their might, revealing a hole and a long, greenish line that disappeared into its darkness.

"Woah!" I said. "What's that line thingy?"

"This is no ordinary seaweed, and that *line thingy* is its roots. It leads you all the way to the palace," Queenie said.

"That must be a long line of roots."

"Come, follow us," Millie said as she dived into the hole. Queenie followed after her. I gulped, and then dove in, too.

"It's really dark down here. I can't see a thing!" I exclaimed.

"This secret passageway was built during The Accident so that the royal family could travel wherever they needed without being seen. Their only transportation during that time period was traveling underground," Queenie said. "There are several tunnels underground. But, if you follow the root of the seaweed, it'll take you all the way to the castle."

"Queenie!" Millie screeched.

"Oops!" Queenie smacked her forehead. "Sorry, there's something about her that makes me trust her."

Millie just shook her head. "Paradise, when we arrive, you must treat the royal family with respect. They are the most powerful beings in the ocean . . . and they can do magic of any kind."

"Okay . . ." I said, getting nervous. A few minutes had passed, and I started getting impatient. "How much longer until we get there?"

"We're here now," Queenie said.

The light at the end of the tunnel led straight to the entrance of the castle. There were many mermen holding large spears swimming around it. The castle was a beautiful silver and blue color, but what caught my eye was the big golden R on top.

"What does the R stand for?" I asked. "Oh, wait, Royalty?"

"Yeah," Millie said.

"Human!" one of the palace guards suddenly yelled.

"We must see the royal family immediately!" Millie said.

Another merman, likely the head guard, swam over to us. "Let them in, Krishan. They used the secret tunnel that can only be used in a case of emergency. Plus, they're friends of the royal family." Krishan nodded and went to open the door.

"Sorry about that," the head guard continued. "He's new. Anyways, as it's midday, the royal family will most likely be in their throne room."

As we swam through the palace, there were a few mermaids and mermen swimming around, holding brooms, platters of food, and other items. I could feel all eyes on me. This wasn't the type of attention I wanted. The mermaids gasped in fear and quickly swam away; the mermen followed. When we got to the throne room, the royal family's eyes fell on me in horror. I recognized them from the statue in the city . . . only this time, they weren't looking so upright and proper. Their jaws hung open.

"Guards," the king said. "Leave us. Make sure no one enters the castle." The guards swam out, and I was left with Millie, Queenie, and the royal family.

"Millie, Queenie, who is this?" The queen's blue eyes pierced through me; she had eyes of ice. The entire royal family did. Even though they were the most intimidating family I had ever met, they were also the most gorgeous family. It made me realize that I may not be the prettiest person in the world.

"This is Paradise," Millie said.

"Paradise?" the queen asked as her long brown hair flowed beside her.

"Paradise Jones," Queenie clarified.

"Oh?" the queen said. She eyed me from head to toe.

"How did you enter Aquaria?" the king asked in a deep, stern voice.

"Well, I swam to the bottom of the Blue Grotto, and my necklace started glowing. And then a boulder moved and created a hole, so I swam through," I said truthfully.

"You opened the Changeling Entrance with your necklace?" the queen asked, looking at her husband with wide eyes.

A Changeling Entrance? "Um, yeah. I mean, yes, ma'am," I stuttered.

"Can I see this necklace of yours?" she asked suspiciously.

I reached into the pocket of my swimming shorts, but my necklace was gone. "It's gone!" I exclaimed.

"Imposter!" The king immediately rose from his throne. "You lie. But how did you *know?*"

"Know what?"

"Don't play this game with me, young lady! I'm no fool. I hereby ban you from ever visiting any ocean again." He grabbed his golden scepter with a crystal ball at the top.

"Wait, William," the queen said. "I want to have a full investigation of this. We should keep her down here longer to see how she got in, so that we can make sure this never happens again."

"But she could be dangerous," the king added.

"She's a harmless teenager," Queenie said. "We already investigated her."

"What? When?" I asked, confused.

The queen looked at me. "You are dealing with the smartest mermaids in the whole kingdom. We royalty are very intelligent, and although they are only eleven, Millie and Queenie are much cleverer than you think. You can't, and won't, fool any of us."

The three princesses and prince stared at me.

"In the meantime," one of the princesses began, "Millie, Queenie, keep an eye on her. Find her some friends her age who won't be afraid of her. We'll send a message out to all of Aquaria to say that she's not harmful."

"Yes, Your Highness," Millie and Queenie said in unison and bowed. I followed them out.

"That was stressful," I told them as we were swimming back to the town. "But the royal family is beautiful! They have the most gorgeous brown hair . . . even prettier than mine. And their eyes. Oh my! Don't even get me started on their eyes."

"They are a beautiful family," Queenie agreed. "And their eye color is representative of being a part of the royal family. You won't find anyone else in the ocean with eyes like that."

"That's so cool. I've always wanted blue eyes!" I said. "What are all of their names? I mean, I have a feeling they're going to want to see me quite a few more times."

"Well, the king and queen are King William and Queen Christiana. The oldest princess, who's twenty-one, is Princess Torrie," Millie said.

"Is she the one with the braid leading to a bun?" I asked.

I paid close attention to hair, obviously.

"Yes," Millie said. "Princess Tatiana is the one with the long ponytail. She is eighteen. Then, the young princess, Princess Penelope, well it's obvious who she was. She was the tiny one with curly hair. She's five. Then, there's the boy, Prince Alexander. He's three."

"Wow, there are so many of them," I said.

"Quick, get behind us!" Queenie suddenly said.

I swam behind them. "What? What's wrong?" I whispered.

"News narwhals, we can't let them see you," Queenie said. "We need the merfolk to hear from the royal family that there is a human down here. We can't let the news spread from them."

After a long while of swimming, we finally got back to the main city. I noticed that the shops were filled with newspapers that seemed to be all about me. I was shocked at how the news had reached the town square before we had. Millie and Queenie explained to me that the machines in Aquaria are much faster and more developed than they are in the human world. A picture of me was on the front page. Below it, the article read:

The Narwhal Newspaper

"Human girl, known as Paradise Jones, intrudes into Aquaria. While she isn't a threat and appears harmless, we have to keep her down here to see how she got in." —Queen Christiana

"Jones came through one of the Changeling Entrances. We still don't know how, but we are sending guards to each entrance to secure them, just in case." —King William

"All merfolk must stay aware. There is no reason to be frightened of this human—she's merely a teenager—but keep your eyes peeled just in case we have other humans slipping past the newly stationed guards." —Princess Torrie

"She seems pretty cool to me. Try to make friends with her; find out what her interests are." —Princess Tatiana

"She reminds me of my mommy." —Princess Penelope

"Pretty hair." —Prince Alexander

"This is The Accident all over again! Our worst nightmare has come true! This girl is here to kill us all and expose our kind! We are DOOMED!" —Gossiping Goosefish

"Wow," I finally said, in shock. "I've always wanted to be famous, but definitely not like this."

As we entered the main square, mermaids were staring at me wide-eyed as they were passing by. Why were they freaking out? I should've been freaking out! I was among half-human, half-fish!

"We're here," Millie said. She led me into a small store called the Coral Café. Everyone sipping their coffee stopped to take a look at me. Most of the merfolk swam out, but two girls who looked my age stayed.

"The royal family would like you two to watch over Paradise as the investigation is going on. Take care of her," Queenie said.

"Wait—you're leaving me?"

"You're in good hands," Millie assured. "We need to go back and discuss this with the royal family. See you soon, Paradise."

She and Queenie swam away.

"Uh, hi . . . " I started.

"Hi!" the mermaid with strawberry-blonde hair said. "This is so cool! Nothing this exciting has happened . . . in a while. I'm from the Dolphin family. My name is Delfina."

I cracked a smile and tried not to laugh. "Delfina Dolphin."

"Yeah, kind of a funny name, I know. But don't worry, my parents aren't dolphins!" she reassured.

The other mermaid had tan skin and long, jet black hair.

She extended her arm out. "I'm from the Marine family. My name is Aqua."

"Woah, your name is Aqua Marine? That's pretty cool," I said and shook her hand.

Aqua smiled. "Tell us a little about yourself."

"Well, I think you should know that I'm a harmless teenage girl. I'm sixteen and live in Los Angeles, California. I go to a school called Charm High, and my best friend, Zahara, and I are the most popular girls in school. We want to be models when we grow up."

"Wow! I've always wanted to see the human world," Delfina said. "We're sixteen, too. Aqua and I are best friends and go to Seahorse High School. At our school, there isn't really popularity. Everyone is friends, and we all want to make the ocean a better place."

"Delfina and I love adventures," Aqua said. "We love exploring Aquaria during our free time. We've explored almost every inch of the city. So, you coming here is like another adventure for us!"

"Wow, that's really cool," I said. I'd always been interested in adventuring in the mall, but not anywhere else. Aqua and Delfina seemed to have a lot more knowledge about their world than I did about mine, which made me curious to start experiencing other places besides the mall.

"So, have you been on a tour of Aquaria yet?" Aqua asked.

"Seeing that most mermaids and mermen seem to be scared of me, and the royal family doesn't fully trust me . . . no."

"Oh my gosh! We have to show you around," Delfina said. "You'll love it down here."

"And don't worry about what the merfolk think of you," Aqua said. "They're just nervous because you remind them of The Accident."

"What even is The Accident?" I asked.

"I think once we get to know you better, we'll tell you . . ." Delfina's voice trailed off. "But for now, come on! We have so much to show you."

I couldn't believe I was about to go on a tour of a mermaid world. Rosie and I had always wished we were mermaids so that we could swim away and leave Pauvres-Kalai forever, and now my dreams of meeting a mermaid were coming true.

CHAPTER 6

Aquatic Adventures

As we were swimming through the huge town, merfolk were giving me dirty looks.

"I heard she's helping a sea witch in the Deep Crevice," one mermaid said.

"Really? The Gossiping Goosefish told me she's out here to expose all mermaids and get us killed!" another one said.

I gulped and kept following Aqua and Delfina.

"First things first," Delfina said. "We're going to get you a shell phone!"

"A shell phone?" I laughed. "Did you know up where I live, we call them cell phones?"

"Actually, yes, the changelings tell us all about your world," Aqua said.

My world. "What are changelings?"

"Changelings are merfolk who can transform into humans. Only a handful of us can transform," Aqua said.

"And what does it mean when they say I came through a Changeling Entrance?" I asked.

"The changelings can only go through certain entrances and exits. The entrances only open on one Sunday every month. So, you can leave on a Sunday in July and come back to the entrance later in the day. Or, you can leave on a Sunday in July and come back on a Sunday in August. And, it's a new rule that on those Sundays each month, the entrances get closed down to humans," Delfina explained.

"So that's why the Blue Grotto was closed when I came," I said. "But the merfolk can't just go up and say 'Oh the mermaids and mermen would like to come back now. Close the Grotto.' Can they?"

"That's why we sent a changeling to work as the head of each Changeling Entrance. They can choose when to close it," Delfina said.

"Oh, that's smart."

"But we still don't know how you got in," Aqua pondered aloud. "The changeling at the Blue Grotto must have not been trustworthy because he let you in, and changelings have special lockets that allow them to enter through the different entrances."

"I have a locket," I said.

"You do? But how?" Delfina asked, surprised.

"I've always had it. My real parents left it for me before they dropped me off at an orphanage," I said sadly. "Are you guys changelings?"

"We wish," they replied in unison.

"How do you determine if you are or not?"

"Well, the royal family is automatically born with the power of being a changeling. Although, they don't like to risk their lives in the human world, so they rarely ever go up there. They've only used the Changeling Entrance twice. As for other merfolk, you just randomly have that power when you are born," Delfina said.

"Well, do you think I'm a changeling?" I asked.

"You say you have a locket and you're breathing under-water, so there's something special about you," Aqua said. "But I don't think you could be a changeling because you still have legs, and you would've transformed into a mermaid by now if you were."

"Say, do you have that locket of yours?" Delfina asked.

"I lost it," I groaned.

"Well, look on the bright side, we're here at Shelly's Shell Phones!" Delfina exclaimed.

As we swam into the store, there were rows and rows of different kinds of shells. They came in different colors, shapes, and sizes. I was immediately attracted to the cream-colored conch shell phone. I didn't have any money—obviously—but Aqua and Delfina were kind enough to pay with their "mermoney" as they called it.

I was confused why there weren't any numbers on the shell phone to dial. But down here in this magical world, all you had to do was say the name of the person you wanted to call into the opening of the shell. Pretty cool, right? They didn't have any social media on their phones, but there was a store called Finstagram & Crabchat where you could go and take pictures of yourself and have them posted in the store for a day. *So weird.*

"So, there are three major spots every merfolk likes to visit. Finstagram & Crabchat, Water World, and the Deep Crevice," Delfina said.

"Those sound like cool places. What are they? Can we go to Water World and the Deep Crevice today, too?" I asked.

"Water World is an amusement park, so of course we can go there," Aqua said. "But we are not going to the Deep Crevice. It's a deep, dark crack in the ground in the country-side of Aquaria. Merfolk who venture down there to see what kinds of creatures lie within never return. Ever."

"Yeah, even though Aqua and I are adventurous, we don't want to risk our lives!" Delfina exclaimed.

"So then why would merfolk want to see it?" I asked.

"It's just a creepy sightseeing place. Merfolk don't go into the actual crevice anymore. They look from above, some-times hang out for a little bit there, and then leave," Aqua explained.

"Oh. Well in that case, let's just go to Water World."

After a few minutes of swimming, we arrived.

"Well, hello there," a mermaid with a strange, heavy accent said at the ticket booth of Water World. "Ahhh! The human!"

"Three tickets, please," Aqua said, ignoring her.

The mermaid quickly handed us our tickets. When we entered, it looked just like a typical amusement park . . . only, it was underwater. There were plenty of rides similar to those back home in Disneyland, but they were called funny names like Mad Sea Party, Fairytail Adventures, Krilliant Koaster, and more. The first ride we went on was a large Ferris wheel, and from the top we could see all of Aquaria. The palace was huge, and the town square was buzzing with mermaids and mermen. Then, we went on the Krilliant Koaster, a roller-coaster that passed through one of the strongest currents in Aquaria. Afterward, I was feeling a little seasick, so we went on Fairytail Adventures. We sat in clam shells that slowly took us through the history of Aquaria. Since it was a slow and calming ride through history, I thought it was a good opportunity to see if Aqua and Delfina would tell me about The Accident.

"So, any chance you'll tell me about The Accident now?" I pleaded as we rode.

"Paradise, we can't," Aqua said sadly. "We trust you, but if the other merfolk found out you know about it, they'd be furious."

"Why won't you tell her? It's not that big of a deal," I heard a voice say from behind me in another clam. I turned around and felt my body tingle. The mermaid behind us had large green eyes, light-brown skin, and long, curly, golden locks. She seemed to be in her mid-twenties. "I'll tell you, if you'd like."

The ride came to an end, and we all swam off.

"But the royal family—" Delfina started.

"I can tell you everything." The mermaid stuck out her hand. "I'm from the Shark family."

"I'm from the Jones family," I said, slowly shaking her hand. "My name is—"

"Paradise, I know. We all do. I'm Sharika."

"Hi, Sharika Shark," I said. "You can tell me *everything*?"

"Yes, Paradise, I can."

"But how? Why?" I asked. Why would this random stranger want to help me?

"Let's just say I'm familiar with these waters," Sharika said.

"What is that supposed to mean?" Delfina asked. "Sharika, just leave us alone."

Delfina grabbed my and Aqua's arms and swam away.

"Why wouldn't you let her tell me?" I asked.

"Honestly, she's a bit strange," Delfina said. "She just appeared here one day about five years ago. She hasn't told us where she's from, and she doesn't even have any friends. Right, Aqua?"

"She's right," Aqua said. "Just stay away from her."

I sighed and agreed. They knew more about the mermaids down here than I did or ever would.

After we spent the rest of the afternoon around town, I went to have a sleepover at Delfina's house. Unfortunately,

Aqua said she couldn't make it. Delfina told me she studied a lot at nights, so she could never really go to sleepovers. Delfina and I swam to the hoop portals, and she typed in her address: 43110 Starfish Street, Dolphin Family House. I swam aside so the hoop could scan her, and then we swam in together. When I swam out of the ring, I was in a neighborhood. *How cool is that?!* We ended up right in front of her pink coral house.

Each family had their own hoop outside of their house. Delfina explained to me that when you swam through this hoop, it would lead you to a store filled with the "exit circles" of all the families. The exit circles led you back into the town square.

Her neighbors looked at me in horror and quickly swam into their coral homes. I sighed and swam into Delfina's house. Her parents weren't home yet, so we swam upstairs. Her bed was made out of seaweed; I thought it was disgusting. I wondered where I would sleep . . . *wait a second.*

"Delfina, what time is it?" I asked frantically.

"Five o'clock. Why?" she asked.

"I totally forgot about the human world! I have to be back at my boat by 5:15! I'll never make it in time!" I panicked.

Delfina thought quickly. "Um . . . oh! Your shell phone—you can call your parents!"

"I can call humans?" I asked. "Well, okay . . . Paul Jones," I said into the opening of my conch shell phone. It started vibrating.

"Hello?"

"Dad?" I asked.

"Paradise? Where are you?" Dad asked. "The call came up as the location of 'Unknown Waters.'"

"Oh, that's strange. I'm at Capri still . . . I fell asleep on the beach! Must be my jet lag. I'm going to be a little late."

"Okay. Thanks for letting me know. Hurry up."

I breathed out heavily. "Sorry, Delfina, I totally forgot! Let's do this sleepover another time."

"No problem! Here, you can travel through my circle to get back to the town square," she replied.

We swam out of her house, and I waved goodbye. I swam through her hoop and ended up in a store full of the family hoops in the town square.

"Ahhh!" I screamed. Millie and Queenie were right in front of me.

"We were waiting to see how long it would take for you to remember about your world," Millie said.

"Come on, we'll swim you back to the Changeling Entrance!" Queenie exclaimed.

They started swimming rapidly out of the store, and I followed. When we arrived near the entrance, Queenie told me that it was 5:13. We were pretty fast swimmers. Now that I could breathe while swimming, I was even faster! Now, if it takes you two minutes to swim across a pool, it'll take me fifteen seconds!

"Here is the entrance to the Blue Grotto. Farewell,

Paradise," Millie said.

"Wait!" Queenie exclaimed. She quickly dove down behind a kelp bed and dragged me and Millie down with her. "There are guards at the entrances. Doesn't the royal family want Paradise to stay down here until we figure out how she got in?"

"I've already spoken with the royal family. I got them to agree to let Paradise go home for the night. If she doesn't, her family will worry about her, which would not be good for Aquaria if they start looking for her around the Grotto. But if she's not back here tomorrow morning, changeling guards will be sent to find her," Millie said.

"But my locket is gone! How will I get in?" I asked.

They both tilted their heads. "Paradise, are you sure you got in with a locket? Because only changelings have lockets . . . " Queenie said.

"I've had that locket since I was a baby, and I'm pretty sure it's what let me into Aquaria."

"Well, we'll be waiting here at nine o'clock when the guard will open the entrance for you," Millie said. "The Blue Grotto opens up for tourists at 9:30 am. Do not be late."

I nodded, and one of the guards opened the entrance for me to swim through. I waved goodbye and swam all the way back up to air. It was sunset, and I was alone.

CHAPTER 7

Back to Reality

Being back in reality was weird. I was only in Aquaria for a few hours, but I really felt a connection to the place more than I did on land. I didn't dare tell my family, or even Zahara, what I saw. I suspected the royal family was powerful enough to destroy me. Plus, there were so many secrets I still wanted to find out. My mind was racing. *What happened to my locket? How did I enter a mermaid world with the necklace my real parents gave me? Why did King William ask how I "know?" Know what? What was The Accident? What was in the Deep Crevice that kept making adventuring merfolk disappear? Why did Sharika Shark want to help me?*

"How was your day, Paradise?" Sam asked me when we were at dinner. I had only gotten back five minutes late.

"It was great. I ended up just swimming and sleeping on the beach the entire time!" I lied. "Mom, Dad, is there any way I can go back tomorrow? I never got to shop!"

"I mean, it was kind of nice with just the three of us . . . " Mom said. Ouch.

"Sheila only gave you today to use her yacht, though, and we are not paying that much for you to go back to Capri," Dad said.

Suddenly, my phone buzzed.

Unknown: Hello, Paradise! How was your day?

Me: Who is this?

Unknown: Sheila! Remember? Sheila Meela?

Me: Ohhh. Yes. It was great! I had the best time ever! ☺

I knew I had to be nice in order to get her yacht for a few more days.

Sheila: I'm so glad to hear that. I would've joined you, but I got food poisoning! I'm going to have to stay in another day.

Me: OMG! That sucks! I was wondering, is there any possible way I could use your yacht again tomorrow? . . .

Sheila: Of course! As long as you are going to Capri again.

Me: That's the plan.

Sheila: Excellent! I should be better after tomorrow, and then I will come with you!

Oh no. I couldn't take her with me! How would I escape her for the whole day? I couldn't make up that many excuses!

Me: Sounds good!

"Sheila's letting me use her yacht again!" I squealed. Mom glared at me. Why was she so jealous? She just said that she liked being with just her real family.

"You're welcome," Sam said. "I gave her your number. She asked for it. I almost didn't because you're an annoying little sister."

I rolled my eyes and laughed. "Thanks!"

Mom snarled. What was up with her?

After eating, we went straight back to the room. I was exhausted. I ran and jumped into bed. Instead of falling asleep right away, I lay there thinking about all the things that had happened in the past couple days. I met Rihanna and Sheila Meela. I discovered a mermaid world. I met two of the smartest mermaids, Millie and Queenie Reef. I met the royal family of Aquaria: King William, Queen Christiana, Princess Torrie, Princess Tatiana, Princess Penelope, and Prince Alexander. I made two new friends, Aqua Marine and Delfina Dolphin. And finally, I met a strange mermaid named Sharika Shark, who wanted to tell me everything I wanted to know. And, wow, I remembered all of their names.

"Megan, you are starting to act up a lot more than usual," I heard Dad whisper from the other room.

"I just can't stand her anymore. She is driving me nuts!" Mom said.

"Megan, honey, we adopted her. Paradise is our child now."

"But we didn't even want her!" Mom screeched quietly. My heart stopped. "When her real parents approached us on our vacation in Paris, I thought their offer of gold in exchange for us adopting Paradise was too good to pass up. And then, of course, they threatened to do something horrible to us if we took the gold but didn't adopt her. But I really wanted that gold! I thought at least that we'd be set forever with that much money, but it's just not worth it anymore. *She's* not worth it anymore."

"I know, honey," Dad said quietly. "That's what I thought too, but I didn't know how fast we'd spend that gold. I can't believe it's almost gone."

"And now she is making us pay more for everything when we don't even want to spend money on her. She is getting amazing experiences on Sheila Meela's yacht! Why does she even deserve that?" Mom asked.

Tears started forming in my eyes. I wasn't wanted. I wasn't wanted by anybody. Not by my real parents, and not even by my adoptive parents. That's when I decided: tomorrow night, I was going to pack my stuff and leave the Jones family. Forever. I would sneak out when everyone was asleep, so they wouldn't be able to stop me. I would go to Aquaria, and even if they ended up sending me away, I would move far, far away.

CHAPTER 8

A Day with Royalty

I woke up early and told my parents that I'd be gone for a little longer than yesterday. I didn't care if they tried to fight with me about timing, I wasn't going to listen. I sailed back to Capri early in the morning and had my captain wait at the dock for me. I told him I'd be back at 6:30 p.m. After he docked, I went over to the beach and swam out far so no one could see me. I dipped my head into the cool ocean water and swam all the way to the Blue Grotto. I swam all the way to the bottom, and as they promised, Millie and Queenie were there waiting for me.

"I hate the human world," I said as I swam through the entrance.

"Well, good morning to you, too," Queenie said. "Life down under is much better."

"Wait—how were you able to open the entrance? Are you girls changelings?" I asked.

"Yes," they said at the same time.

"But remember, we told you the guard would open it up," Millie said, pointing to the serious-looking merman guarding the entrance.

"Oh, right. My brain is a little tired. I couldn't fall asleep last night," I said. "Anyways, where to first? Can I go back with Aqua and Delfina?" I asked.

"Before you do, the royal family wants to have you over for breakfast," Millie said.

I gulped. They started swimming away, and I followed. As we got to the town square, I heard a large gasp. When I turned around, I saw a large, brown fish with a wide mouth. It was the Gossiping Goosefish.

"Paradise! Paradise! Is it true you want to use us all as samples for science?" the Gossiping Goosefish asked.

"No! Why would I want to do that? Humans are mean and selfish people!" I exclaimed.

The Gossiping Goosefish quickly swam away into *The Narwhal Newspaper* headquarters.

Queenie rolled her eyes. "Ignore her; she just wants as much gossip as she can get."

A few minutes later, we were still swimming but had yet to reach the palace.

"How much longer?" I groaned. "Why couldn't we just take the secret sand passageways?"

"Those are only for emergencies, Paradise," Millie said.

As we finally approached the palace, the newbie guard,

Krishan, looked at me strangely again. "Human! Oh wait, it's you again. Come on in."

The gates were opened, and I swam through by myself. The palace was huge, but I just trailed after the smell of the delicious breakfast.

"Ah, Paradise, good morning," Princess Torrie said when I reached the dining room. "Please, take the seat across from my mother." The table was a rectangle, and I swam to sit at the end of it.

"How are you enjoying Aquaria?" Queen Christiana asked me.

"I love it. I feel more at home down here than up in the human world," I said. Her icy blue eyes wouldn't leave mine.

"Do you play any sports?" Princess Tatiana asked.

"No."

"Do you like school? We have a tutor come here for us," Princess Penelope said. She was adorable.

"No, I don't really like school."

"What do you want to be when you grow up?" Princess Torrie asked.

"A world-famous model," I said. "Just like Sheila Meela. Have you heard of her?"

The king and queen stiffened.

"Yes," King William said.

"A model?" Princess Torrie said. "Shouldn't you do something educational and have modeling as a side job? Very few models actually succeed."

"I'm surprised your family doesn't model," I said truthfully. "I've never seen such a pretty family. My family . . . "

"Tell us about your family," Queen Christiana interjected.

"They're the worst," I said. "You see, I'm adopted."

Queen Christiana sat up straighter. "You don't like your parents?"

"My parents are the worst parents you could ever imagine. I mean, the only reason they take me on these vacations is because of their son. They can't just leave me at home. But they are awful. They treat me like . . . like I'm not a part of the family." Queen Christiana gave me a puzzled look and shrunk back down into her seat.

"So, they're vile?" Princess Torrie said with fire in her eyes.

"What does 'vile' mean?" Prince Alexander asked.

"It means unpleasant and cruel, son," King William explained. Prince Alexander still looked puzzled.

"It means they're meanies," Princess Tatiana said and stuck out her tongue. Prince Alexander laughed. Princess Torrie rolled her eyes.

Waiters entered the room to serve us breakfast. It was just like a breakfast you'd have at a five-star hotel. There were delicious-looking pastries, jams, and clotted cream, platter after platter. At the end of the line of waiters stood a huge, purple narwhal.

The look of shock on my face caused Princess Tatiana to explain, "Don't be scared. He's just a News Narwhal. He comes to hear our feedback on the local news so he can put our opinions into the newspaper every day."

The News Narwhal took out a notepad. "Hello, Your Highnesses. What would you like to say for *The Narwhal News-paper* today? We're reporting about Paradise." He gave me a quick glance and then looked back at the royals.

"She's just a harmless, young teenager who aspires to be a model," Princess Torrie said.

"She seems fine. Everyone just needs to chill out," Princess Tatiana added.

"She has no parents," Princess Penelope confirmed. The whole family shot her a look. "I mean, she has no parrots!"

"What are parrots?" the News Narwhal asked.

"They're these animals in the human world," Princess Torrie said.

"She wants to be like Sheila Meela," said Prince Alexander to the News Narwhal. King William, Queen Christiana, and Princess Torrie looked horrified. I didn't know why, and I bet Prince Alexander had no clue, either.

The News Narwhal winced.

"You may *not* put that in there," Queen Christiana said, her eyes angry. "Put instead that she wants to be a model."

The News Narwhal gulped and scribbled on his notepad. The rest of the time, the king and queen just said how they still hadn't figured out how I entered the Changeling Entrance even though I told them it was because of my locket. They didn't believe me. I had no locket to show them. It was still lost, and they had sent out search parties to find it. If the search parties didn't find it, they said they would be convinced I was lying and I could be severely punished.

After we finished breakfast, they said they wanted their children to get to know me more. I guessed it was some kind of test to make sure that I was safe. They even stationed a guard in each of their bedrooms to make sure I wouldn't do any harm or human witchcraft. I tried to explain that magic doesn't even exist in the human world, but they weren't too convinced. I started in Prince Alexander's room. He had a small room with blue painted walls and a crib with gold starfish hanging above it.

"Well, um, what would you like to do?" I asked awkwardly. Suddenly, my shell phone began to ring.

"Who's it?" he asked me.

Out of the opening of the conch shell, a voice said, "Zahara Henderson."

I took the shell phone and put it to my ear. "Hello?"

"Paradise," Zahara said angrily.

"Hey, bestie!" I said.

"Don't you 'hey, bestie' me! You haven't talked to me in ages!"

"It's been, like, two days," I said.

"Yeah, well, you haven't even asked me how I like New York . . . " she said sadly.

"OMG! How is New York?" I asked.

"It's amazing. Jayla did a great job planning our trip.

Paradise, why does your voice sound like that?"

"Like what?"

"It sounds all bubbly and weird. You know those apps that make you sound like you're talking underwater? Like that," she said.

"Oh, weird. Maybe it's just the reception. International calls, you know," I lied.

"So, where are you?"

"Paradise, hurry uuuup," Prince Alexander started whining.

"Who is that?" Zahara asked.

"Uh, just this random kid on our yacht . . ." I started.

"What's a yacht?" Prince Alexander asked.

"Huh?" Zahara asked.

"Prince A . . . I mean—" *Oh shoot.* She couldn't know I was hanging out with a prince! "Prince, you know what a yacht is. We're on one right now."

"His name is Prince?" Zahara asked.

"Prince? My name is Alexander," Prince Alexander said to me.

"Alexander? Who's Alexander?" Zahara asked. "Paradise, do you have a boyfriend? How could you not tell me?"

"Paradise has a boyfriend!" Prince Alexander chanted.

"OMG, you totally have been lying to me!" Zahara exclaimed.

"Liar, liar! Pants on fire!" Prince Alexander chanted.

"Even that little boy, Prince, thinks you're a liar!" Zahara started laughing.

"Zahara, I do not have a boyfriend. And this little boy wants me to go play with him. I'll catch up with you later?"

"Fine, Paradise." Zahara hung up the phone. Okay, so now she was mad? She was just laughing a second ago. Honestly, her mood swings could get very confusing!

I turned to Prince Alexander. "Thanks a lot for that."

He giggled. "Let's play with blocks!"

I sat down and started playing blocks with him. He wanted to know what it was like where I came from, so I built him what my house looked like. He told me it was pretty and asked me to build more. I actually enjoyed spending time with a three-year-old. It was like being with the little brother I never had. We played for about an hour until the guard escorted me to Princess Penelope's room. Her room was pink and had huge stuffed animals everywhere. She was sitting on the floor and had a tea set out.

"Hi, Paradise!" She waved. "Welcome to my tea party!"

"Wow, it looks very delicious," I said. I sat down next to her. She stared at me and didn't say anything. "What's wrong?"

"You didn't say hello to the other guests." She pointed at her stuffed animals and mermaid dolls. "That is very rude."

"Oh, I am so sorry," I said, trying not to laugh. "Hello, guests of Princess Penelope."

"Paradise, you are one of my best friends now," Princess Penelope said.

"I am?"

"Yes. I've only invited a few mermaids to my tea parties. And since I invited you, you can just call me Penelope!"

I felt so honored. "Oh, wow! Thanks, Penelope."

"Do you like my hair?" she asked. "I made it extra special just for you."

It was the same bouncy brown curls as yesterday. "It's lovely."

She poured me a glass of tea. "Cheers! To Princess Paradise!"

"Princess?" I asked.

"You are as pretty as a princess," Penelope said and clinked her tea cup against mine. I took a sip. "You can't drink until you click tea cups with my dollies!"

I bit my cheeks to refrain from laughing. Her big, icy blue eyes wouldn't leave mine until I did what she asked.

"You have very pretty eyes," I said.

"Thank you! Me and Mommy and Daddy and Torrie and Tatiana and Alexander all have the exact same eyes. We're the only merfolk in all of Aquaria who have blue eyes."

I smiled and took a sip of my tea. After I finished the tea party with Penelope, I was led to Princess Tatiana's room. It was filled with posters of famous human and mermaid athletes. It looked like a sports magazine had thrown up all over her walls.

"Hi, Princess Tatiana," I said and swam in, looking around.

"Please, just call me Tatiana," she said. She thumped down on her bed. "So, what's the latest and greatest?"

"Well, just that everyone thinks that I'm here to take all of your lives," I said.

"Personally, I don't believe any of that. You seem harmless to me," Tatiana said and bit into a cookie. "Want some?"

I shook my head. "So, you're into sports?"

She immediately sprung up and started swimming around her room. "Paradise, sports are everything to me. I love every sport there is. I play them all! I love going out into the city and playing with the children and challenging merfolk my age. I'm not very princessy, obviously."

"Wow. I wish I were that passionate about sports, but I'm that passionate about modeling."

"Modeling, huh? That's cool. Honestly, the merfolk down here who say they want to be models are so full of themselves. They think they are gorgeous. But the merfolk who should be models and don't know it are the true, beautiful ones."

I was taken aback by this. Was I really full of myself? "Oh."

"Wait, I didn't mean you are full of yourself! I'm just saying, from personal experience, that's how mermaids and mermen are," Tatiana said quickly. "I've never met any humans who want to be models, besides you."

"I think your family should model. You're all gorgeous."

"Thanks!" Tatiana said awkwardly.

Tatiana seemed pretty uncomfortable. I could tell talking

about modeling wasn't really her thing, so I decided to ask her one of my many questions. "Tatiana, you seem pretty adventurous. Have you ever been down in the Deep Crevice?"

"No, never. It's way too dangerous. I'm not allowed."

"Why is it dangerous?" I asked.

She got closer to me and lowered her voice. "No one is really sure, but the legend is that a monster lives in the Deep Crevice. It feeds on anything that goes down there."

I gulped, but then she stopped telling me about the horrors within Aquaria and taught me all about the merfolk sports instead. When they played soccer, they kicked the ball with their tails. They also played handball, and a form of basketball. Instead of dribbling, they just passed the ball around. Tatiana told me her favorite sport was the mermaid version of track; it's a race on a track field for whoever swims the fastest.

Tatiana told me she always wins, and she wanted to race me to see how fast I was. I couldn't say no to a princess, so we raced in the castle gardens. I chased after her rapid tail while looking at the colorful sea anemone around us. As I was looking around, a large balcony caught my eye. I saw Queen Christiana watching us, but once we made eye contact, she turned around and swam back into her room. When I looked back ahead of me, I noticed Tatiana had almost made it out of the garden. I kicked my legs as hard as I could and caught up with her. Surprisingly, I almost beat Tatiana; I was only one second behind her. She was shocked and told me I should join the swim team in the human world. Maybe she was right.

After hanging out with Tatiana for a while, I headed over to Princess Torrie's room. It was a large, clean, cream-colored room. On her desk lay a quill and samples of different sea rocks. There were large scrolls of paper with writing scribbled all over. I'd never seen that much writing in my life, not even from Ms. Art in English class. There was a huge window overlooking the city of Aquaria. I could see Finstagram & Crabchat, Shelly's Shell Phones, Water World, and even a bit of the Deep Crevice. I slowly swam in. Tatiana said Princess Torrie was very bossy and strict, so I should be careful of what I said.

"Hello, Paradise," Princess Torrie said.

"Hi," I said slowly. I looked over at her desk.

"That's my researching desk. Since I am the future queen of Aquaria, I am very interested in knowing every aspect about it. I need to make it the safest and best it can be."

"So you research rocks and bits of coral reefs?" I asked. It seemed like a boring science class to me.

"Not just any rocks and coral. I take only special kinds. For example, this is a piece of silver I found in the secret sand passageways underground. I examine every inch of it, do tests, and write down all the recordings I can find."

"Well, how interesting," I lied.

"I know you're lying," Princess Torrie said. "I am one of

the smartest in the family. You can't fool me. I'm going to find out just how you got into Aquaria."

"Princess Torrie, I've told you. I came in with a locket."

"That's not possible. The only way to get through is with a changeling locket, which you claim got lost. But I will find out how this really happened. This is the second time."

I wanted to ask her what she meant, but Tatiana said to choose what I said wisely, so I just continued to ask her about her research.

"What's this?" I asked, pointing to a piece of red coal.

"It was found in the Deep Crevice," she said. "Not at the bottom, of course, but I think it floated up from the bottom. One of the guards found it at the top and brought it to me. I'm still trying to figure out why it's red . . . "

"Maybe someone painted it?"

"No. I tried chipping it off at first because I thought it was paint, but it's not. And we don't have any red coal down here in Aquaria." Princess Torrie narrowed her eyes and pondered.

"Maybe someone used magic and changed it red?"

"Impossible. Only the royal family knows how to use magic."

"Well then, I'm out of ideas," I said.

"Paradise, have you ever seen anything like this in the human world?"

"Never. Coal is black and glows red when it's hot. It's never just a solid red color."

"Strange," Princess Torrie said. She then sat on her desk and started writing more notes. I awkwardly just floated there until she was done. "So, you want to be a model?"

"Yeah, I really want to," I replied.

"Why not a doctor? Or a lawyer? Or a businesswoman?" she asked. Why was everyone against models?

"None of those things really call out to me. I'm not really a school kind of person. Might as well put my beaut—" I paused, not wanting to sound obnoxious, "my love for the runway and having photoshoots to good use. Plus, it's too late to start trying in school. I'm in the lowest classes possible. And even if I joined the swim team, I'd be going into it as a newbie eleventh grader, so it's not like I could get an athletic scholarship."

"It is never too late to start trying," Princess Torrie said passionately. "You have your whole life ahead of you. Don't let negative people or unwillingness stand in your way."

"Negative people?" I asked.

"Didn't you say you don't like your family?"

"I mean, I don't; except for my brother, Sam. They know I want to be a model, so they are always bringing me down."

"Listen, Paradise. If your parents are bringing you down, rise above them! The only thing that should be able to pull you that far down under is the monster in the Deep Crevice."

"That was deep," I said sarcastically. Princess Torrie looked annoyed. "Deeply enriching! Thanks for the pep talk, Torrie . . . I mean, Princess Torrie. My bad!"

"Torrie" just flowed so much more naturally for me than "Princess Torrie."

Princess Torrie just shook her head. Luckily, the guard saved me from the awkwardness and told me I could leave. I said goodbye to Princess Torrie, Tatiana, Penelope, and Prince Alexander and left. King William and Queen Christiana were busy doing royal things, so I just left without saying goodbye to them. I was sure they'd want me to come over again for another interrogation. Millie and Queenie were waiting outside the palace for me and were ready to swim me back to the town square.

Today, they were wearing their hair differently. They matched yesterday, and I could barely tell them apart. Today, Millie just let her short, blonde hair flow at her shoulders, but Queenie had hers in a braid. I still couldn't believe I was in an underwater fantasy. It was like Rosie's and my childhood dreams of being the Little Mermaid were coming true!

As we swam into the town square, many of the merfolk were reading *The Narwhal Newspaper*. What everyone had said at breakfast was on the front page. Unfortunately, the Gossiping Goosefish decided to include another lie in the paper: "The girl is here to expose us and make us all samples to human scientists! I heard her say it myself!" The merfolk were all looking at me with threatening or worried looks. I just shook my head and kept swimming along. My legs were becoming sore from kicking around so much. I just wished I could have a tail.

Suddenly, someone said, "Paradise, hey." I looked up. It was Sharika Shark.

"Hi, Sharika," I replied. Her eyes looked like they had a faint red ring around them, but I was probably just seeing things. I wasn't used to having my eyes open in salt water for hours on end. "Millie, Queenie, thanks for bringing me back. I'll catch up with you guys later?"

They looked at me and then Sharika, nodded skeptically, and swam away. Sharika must have noticed me staring at her eyes in a funny way. "What's wrong?"

"Nothing! Just that there are red rings around your eyes, I think . . . " I started.

She took out a mini-mirror and looked at herself. "Paradise, I think you're seeing things. There's nothing there."

I rubbed my eyes. "Oh, sorry."

"It's alright! Anyways, I was wondering, do you want to take a light swim to the Deep Crevice with me?" she asked.

I shuddered. "Why the Deep Crevice?"

"Well, I wanted to talk to you, and it's the farthest destination away from here. So, we'll have a lot of time to discuss."

"Okay . . . discuss what?"

We started swimming. "Remember how I said I could tell you anything you want to know?"

"Why do you want to help me answer all my questions? Nobody else does."

Sharika dropped her voice. "Paradise, you have a power that I have never seen before. It's very strong."

"Me? There's no way. I'm just a human."

She breathed in. "Your aura is magical, Paradise! I can feel it. From the moment I met you, I knew there was something different about you. Something special."

"So, if I'm connecting the dots correctly, you want me to use my so-called power to help you with something?" I asked.

"No, Paradise. I'm trying to help you. It's for your own good! For your own safety."

"My safety?"

"Paradise, the royal family wants to have you killed."

My stomach dropped. "But why?"

"You're a human! An intruder in their eyes. Since this has happened for the second time, they have no other choice but to kill you. You're just a miserable teenager from what I've heard. You don't know where to turn. The royal family thinks that you're going to want to expose us all so that you can strike it rich and make a luxurious life for yourself!"

"The second time?" I asked. "This has happened before? Did they kill the other person who found Aquaria?"

"All will be answered if you promise to help me fulfill my task."

"So, what exactly is your task?" I asked with a shaky voice.

Tears started to form in Sharika's eyes. "To overthrow the royal family."

"*What?*" I shrieked. "Do you know how much power they have? I've heard that they have a lot, and I would not like to see it being used against me!"

"Yes, but they want to take away an innocent life! Yours! I cannot stand for such a crime. If we use your special power, we will be able to overthrow them and save you!" Sharika pleaded passionately.

Before I could say anything, I felt someone grab my shoulder from behind. "There you are! We've been looking for you everywhere."

I turned around. It was Delfina and Aqua.

"What are you doing with Paradise?" Delfina asked Sharika.

"You girls wouldn't understand," Sharika said. She looked at me and then swam away.

Suddenly, a group of mermen about my age started pointing fingers at me and laughing. Some of them started making faces, and others picked up rocks to start throwing at me.

"Hey!" Aqua said and swam in front of me. "She has done nothing to you. Leave her alone." Her eyes were swimming with anger and her long, black hair was floating all over the place. She looked like a superhero.

The mermen just looked at her and laughed. Suddenly, she picked up one of the rocks and chucked it at one merman's stomach. Within seconds, the merman's eyes teared up. The other mermen looked at Aqua in fear and quickly swam away.

She turned around and rolled her eyes. "Teenage mermen—they think they're the toughest beings in the ocean."

"Come back, and Aqua will ruin one of your pretty faces! Ha!" Delfina yelled to them.

"Thanks, Aqua," I said.

"Anything for my friends," she said and put her arms around us. "So, should we head over to Finstagram & Crab-chat? I'm really loving your swimsuit choice, Paradise. I think we'll get a lot of likes on our picture!"

Delfina nodded, and we started swimming over to Fins-tagram & Crabchat. Here's how it worked: you go to the first screen in the store and take a picture of yourself. It was the same as using Snapchat on your cell phone; you could scroll through filters and everything, but it was on a screen built into a wall instead of on a phone.

After what seemed like a million tries, we finally took the perfect picture. After posting it, the picture was put up on one of the many screens in the store. You could swim around the store and look at other merfolk's pictures while you looked for where yours was posted. The only drawback was that you could only take pictures of yourself in the store; you couldn't take one at your house and then upload it into the store, since everything was taken on a screen. What was also different was that it was like Instagram and Snapchat combined. Our picture would only be up on one of the store's screens for twenty-four hours, but merfolk could like and comment on it. To save the picture, you would just have to print it out. Unfortunately, I couldn't take a copy with me back up to the human world. If that photo got in the hands of the wrong person, Aquaria would be in massive danger.

After having a fun time looking at merfolk's posts in the store, we headed to the Coral Café. We all grabbed a drink and sat down.

"How are you liking Aquaria?" Delfina asked.

"I love it!" I exclaimed. "You guys have been so welcoming."

"It's our pleasure," Aqua said calmly. "You know, we missed school today to help you around."

"Oh, I'm so sorry! Although, if I were you, I wouldn't mind ditching school," I said.

"Ditching?!" Delfina gasped. "We only miss school if we must. Seahorse High School is actually fun."

"We do get a lot of homework, though," Aqua added. "Speaking of which, I need to get going. I have homework to catch up on. I'll see you all tomorrow?"

Delfina and I nodded, and Aqua swam out. "What time are you leaving? I can cram all of my homework in tonight and wait with you now!" Delfina said.

"Oh! Thanks, Delfina." I paused. I knew school was important to her, so I felt bad keeping her behind. "It's okay, though. Go catch up on your homework. If you see Millie and Queenie, ask them if they can come keep me company."

Delfina agreed and waved goodbye. I sat in the café by myself. A cold current of water blew through the door.

"Miss Shark," the café worker said from behind the counter. "I haven't seen you in a while. Would you like your usual?"

"No, thank you. I'm here to speak to Paradise."

CHAPTER 9

The Lonely Mermaid

I gulped. After my last conversation with Sharika about overthrowing the royal family, I was a little nervous to be around her. "Um, hi."

"Paradise, why did you turn so pale?" she asked. "Don't be afraid of me! I realized I came off as intimidating. I just came here to talk."

"Talk about what?"

"I think we should get to know each other better."

"You want to tell me about yourself?" I asked. "My friends said no one knows anything about you."

"That's because I'm a very private person," Sharika said quietly. "I've never told anyone about my past. The merfolk have always judged me. They think I'm a creep!"

"You can tell me about your past . . ."

She took a deep breath. "I come from the Shark family, as you know. We used to live in a different ocean kingdom. It was a very dark place. We lived in a dark cave, and the only way to survive was . . . " Sharika started tearing up.

"It's okay, Sharika. Continue. I won't judge you."

"Thank you, Paradise." She sniffled. "The leader of our ocean kingdom was monstrous. Many years into his ruling, when he started getting old, he cast a spell in order to become immortal. But the only way to remain immortal is to feed off of merfolk blood. In our ocean kingdom, there were only a few families. Us, the Stingray family, the Swordfish family, the Jellyfish family, and the Octopus family. The immortal leader of our ocean kingdom captured us and told us that if we didn't stay and serve him, he would eat us. The only way we would be able to survive was if we brought him a mermaid or merman to eat each day."

"That's horrible! And disgusting," I said.

"It was! Everyone, in each family, took turns bringing a mermaid or merman to him each day from the countryside of nearby ocean kingdoms. Finally, it was my turn. I ventured out and saw a mermaid by herself. It was the perfect opportunity to seize her and take her to our king, but I just couldn't do it; I felt too bad. I abandoned my kingdom and family and never returned after that night. I fled here and have been horrified ever since. I just don't like knowing that my family sacrificed innocent mermaids and mermen to that horrible beast of a king!" Sharika exclaimed.

"Why didn't you ever tell the royal family?" I asked. "They're powerful enough to destroy any being in the ocean!"

"I did!" she cried. "I went to them and told them the same story I told you. They said it wasn't their problem because the merfolk being eaten weren't from Aquaria. Can you believe they just let those poor, innocent lives be taken?"

"I don't believe it!" I said. "And you never told anyone else?"

"No. I was scarred after the royal family completely dismissed the idea. I've always wanted to do something to help my family and the others! Now do you see why I want to overthrow the royal family? They want to kill you, and they won't help these other innocent merfolk being eaten! If we overthrow them, then I can make sure that horrible king gets killed for good. The only way to kill an immortal is to have a king or queen kill him with their magic. And I can make sure you stay alive!"

I took a deep breath. Was this all true? Even after I spent the day with the prince and princesses, they still wanted to kill me? "It still seems so risky . . . "

"I know, I'm sorry. I'm asking too much of you," Sharika said sadly. "It's just that I've never had any friends, and there is something magical about you that makes me want your help!"

"I really want to help you save your family, and, of course, myself! But it's just that the king and queen are so powerful—"

Suddenly, Sharika made a face at something over my shoulder, so I turned around. Millie and Queenie were behind me.

"Hi, Paradise. Hi, Miss Shark," Queenie said suspiciously.

"Paradise, we are here to take you back to the Changeling Entrance," Millie said.

"Oh, right. The human world. Sharika, let's finish talking tomorrow," I said.

Sharika smiled and waved as I left with Millie and Queenie.

"Why were you with Sharika?" Queenie asked as we were swimming back to the entrance.

"Aqua and Delfina had to go do their homework, so Sharika came and kept me company," I said.

"Beware of Sharika Shark, Paradise Jones. There is something fishy about her," Millie said.

"Guys, you don't know her story and background. She really is a good mermaid," I said.

Millie and Queenie remained silent as we got to the entrance. I waved goodbye and told them to not worry about Sharika. She was just misunderstood.

CHAPTER 10

You're Just Like Me

"How was Capri, Paradise?" Sam asked when I got back to the hotel.

"The question should be: how much of my money did you spend shopping and why are you back so late?" Dad asked.

"I actually didn't buy anything. I didn't like anything," I said.

"What's that huge shell in your beach bag?" Mom asked curiously.

It was my shell phone. "I had it with me yesterday. It's a cool shell I found on the beach."

"Why are you carrying it around with you?" she asked nosily.

"It's said to bring good luck," I lied. Mom quickly snatched it from my bag. "There's a crab living in there," I lied again.

"Ugh!" Mom screamed and dropped my shell phone. Thankfully, my quick reflexes allowed me to catch it before it shattered on the floor. I walked into my room before she decided to snatch anything else.

"Mom, where are all of my clothes?" I shrieked.

"I wanted to get Sam's, Paul's, and my clothes laundered. Sam insisted that we launder yours, too." She rolled her eyes. "I did it just for you, Sam. It's wasting our money!"

"What's wasting our money is that you laundered *everything*. I've barely worn any of those clothes!" I whined.

"Oops. Now it looks like you won't be able to come to dinner with us tonight at the five-star restaurant. All of your clothes are being washed! Luckily, ours came back in time." She showed off her fancy dress.

Sam slapped his forehead. "Mommm."

"When will I have my clothes back?" I asked.

"Not until tomorrow. Oopsie!" Mom said with a slight smirk. *Great.* I couldn't run away without any clothes. Now I couldn't leave until tomorrow night.

"Megan, honey, let's go. The car is waiting," Dad said. Sam shook his head and walked out the door. Mom blew me a kiss. "Do not get room service. I'm trying to save money." Dad slammed the door behind them.

Once I couldn't hear their footsteps anymore, I took out my shell phone.

Suddenly, the footsteps started getting loud again. I quickly put the shell phone under my covers. Sam walked back through the door.

"I just wanted to let you know I'm sorry," Sam said sadly. "But, if it makes you feel better, the four of us are going to take a train tomorrow to Rome for the day!"

Nooo!

"Oh, fun," I said and forced a smile. He smiled back and waved bye.

I took my shell phone back out and spoke into it. "Millie Reef." It started ringing.

Millie answered quickly. "Paradise?"

"Millie, I won't be coming tomorrow. My family wants to go to Rome. I'll be there the next day, though!"

"Alright. But you better come back quick. You don't want the royal family to get suspicious," Millie said. If they wanted to kill me, I should've been the one feeling suspicious! But I knew I had to go back. There were still so many mysteries to solve!

"I'll be back as soon as I can, I promise!" I said. Immediately, I texted Sheila.

Me: Hey, Sheila! Thank you soooo much for letting me use your yacht today. I had the best time ever, again!

Sheila: Ah, I am so glad!

Me: I know I'm asking for so much, but this will be the last time. Is it okay if I use it the day after tomorrow?

Sheila: Why not tomorrow?

Me: My parents want to take me to Rome. I don't think they'll want me so far without adult supervision.

Even though my parents didn't love me, I knew now they still had to look out for me. If anything happened, I'm sure my real parents would hunt them down . . . if they were still alive.

Sheila: I'll come along with you to Capri!

Me: Oh! You don't have to do that . . .

Sheila: It's no problem. I'll meet you tomorrow!

Me: Oh, great, thanks.

She couldn't come along with me! I was going to need to devise a plan to make sure she was not with me when I went to the Blue Grotto. I took out a paper and pencil to come up with an idea, but right as the pencil hit the page, I dozed off to sleep.

When I woke up the next the morning, I told my parents that they didn't need to waste their precious money on a train ticket for me to Rome. Dad looked quite pleased, but Mom was suspicious. She asked where I was going and why. I explained to her that Sheila wanted to take me on a personal tour of Capri. She was fuming and immediately told me I couldn't go. Luckily, Dad begged her to let me go with Sheila so that he wouldn't have to pay extra for my day in Rome. After a lot of convincing, she agreed.

Once my laundry arrived, I took a cute pair of clothes and headed outside of the hotel. Sheila and I took her fancy car to where the yacht was docked. We didn't talk the whole drive; she was on a business call for modeling. Honestly, talking on long-winded phone calls about business was not something I was looking forward to. I just wanted to get in there, dress up, take pictures, make my money, and head out. That was all.

"Sorry about that, Paradise," Sheila said when we got to the dock. "It's always business, business, business."

"*Ehi gaurda!*" I heard someone call out from behind me. When I turned around, the man was pointing at Sheila and people immediately started taking their phones out.

"Oh no," Sheila grumbled. "Hey, guys! This is my friend, Paradise. She wants to be a model, too!"

The people looked at me and immediately started screaming and squealing. Sheila quickly hopped on the boat. Where was her bodyguard? These were the times she really needed him. A bunch of girls started running toward me and grabbing my arms. They were all speaking in Italian, but I could make out that they wanted a picture with me. They were yanking me from all sides. One girl nearly ripped my arm out of its socket. Thankfully, Sheila extended her arm out, and I grabbed on and yanked myself onto the boat. My arms were red and covered with fingermarks.

"Owww," I whined as the yacht was pulling into the sea. "Is this what the paparazzi is always like?"

"Even worse, Paradise, even worse."

I sighed and rubbed my arm. "So, Sheila, I think I'm just

going to sleep on the beach all day."

"Oh." She sunk down in her seat. "Alright. There's nothing else you wanted to see?"

"Nope," I said and lay down on the couch. Sheila remained quiet and just looked out into the distance, seeming a little upset.

When we got to Capri, she followed me over to the beach. She just wouldn't leave me alone! After a good hour, when I was fried from the sun, I told her I was going to take a dip in the ocean. She walked over to the shoreline and watched me swim. I swam as far as possible and eventually turned toward the Blue Grotto. It was 9:10; I'd glanced at my cell phone just before diving into the water. I had twenty minutes before the Grotto opened up to tourists. When I looked behind me, I saw someone swimming after me. She was following me!

I picked up my pace, and so did she. I swam all the way to the Blue Grotto. When I poked my head back out of the water, I saw her quickly swimming up behind me. I ducked my head again and swam through the entrance of the cave.

Wait! Oh no. I couldn't get through the Changeling Entrance! *I told Millie and Queenie I wouldn't be coming today. What do I do?* I thought, panicked.

"Paradise! Sheesh, you swim fast," I heard Sheila say from behind me. It was just the two of us at the surface of the water in the Grotto.

"Sheila, why are you following me around everywhere?"

She smiled. "Race you down to the bottom."

She immediately dove down. Oh no! She must not have realized how deep the Grotto really was. I went after her to warn her. I couldn't let her drown! If she did, it would look like I killed her because I was the only person in there with her! And of course, I wouldn't want her to drown, even though she was strange.

I dove down after her. She was extremely quick. I followed her down for minutes on end . . . how did she not run out of breath? When we finally got to the bottom, I was panicked. It was only a matter of time before she drowned. She looked at me. I mouthed the words, "What are you doing?!"

Suddenly, she reached into the pocket of her swimming shorts and pulled out a gold, shiny, heart-shaped necklace. Engraved in it was the name: Sheila Meela. She smiled and held it out toward the crystal. The letters of her name started glowing, her locket popped open, and a ray of light started shooting toward the crystal. Just like my locket had. The big boulder started descending into the ground, but this time, it descended fully into the sand. If my locket was the reason for opening the entrance, maybe the boulder didn't fully descend into the ground because a letter of my last name was scratched off. My mouth hung open in shock. Sheila Meela was a changeling? Was I a changeling? We swam through the entrance.

"You're a changeling?"

"Yes, I am." Sheila smiled.

"Shouldn't you turn into a mermaid, then?"

Sheila sighed deeply. "I can't because of the Ten Years Law."

"What's that?" I asked.

Suddenly, a muscular merman started swimming toward us. I recognized him.

"Paradise, meet my bodyguard, Narayan." Sheila said.

"Narayan . . . don't you work at the palace?" I asked.

"Yes, I am the head guard."

"Your bodyguard is the head guard?" I asked, stunned.

"Paradise, I have so much to explain," Sheila said.

I was assuming she'd begin to explain, but we just swam to the town square in silence. When we got there, many of the merfolk were giving her dirty looks. Narayan got in front of her as we started swimming toward the Coral Café.

"Sheila, why are all of the merfolk looking at you like that?"

She took a deep breath in. "Paradise, it's time for me to tell you a story. Ever since I was a baby, I had this necklace. I never knew my parents, where I was born, or what this necklace meant. All I remember of my parents is their red car, my dad's ivory-colored hair, and my mom's rich brown skin. That's not much to go off of, so I have no idea about their whereabouts today or who they are.

Still, I wore my necklace every day. When I became a famous model, I started to travel the world. Five years ago, I traveled to Greece for a vacation. There was this cave everyone was talking about on the island of Santorini. Being adventurous, I decided to go. At the entrance of the cave, there was a guard. Everyone stood in a line behind him to take a peek into the cave, and then each person left. Legend said that one Sunday of every month, an evil spirit would arise in that cave. That Sunday was the day, so nobody was allowed in. When I got to the front of the line, the guard asked me to step to the side. He waited until everybody had left, and then he let me into the cave. I was so confused!"

"Oh my gosh! He was a changeling, wasn't he?"

Sheila smiled. "I ventured into the cave and found a turquoise pool. Right when I stepped into it, my necklace started glowing and unlocked a Changeling Entrance underwater. I dove down to see what was under there, of course. When I swam through the entrance, there was a sign that pointed in two directions.

In one direction, it said Sealandia, and to the other, it said Aquaria. I gasped with shock that there were signs underwater, and that's when I realized I could breathe underwater. I followed the sign that said Aquaria and after an hour of swimming, I reached the town square. There were merfolk swimming everywhere. When they saw me, the mermaids fainted and the mermen quickly swam back to their homes."

"That's how the merfolk react when they see me!" I exclaimed.

Sheila nodded. "I was immediately escorted by guards to the palace to meet the royal family. They were all horrified to see a human in their waters. I showed them I had a necklace with my name on it and told them it let me into this ocean. They asked me if I was a changeling, and I told them I had no idea what that even meant. They explained to me what a changeling was and that I probably was one. They said there's a Ten Years Law that turns changelings into humans forever if they don't turn into a mermaid or merman for ten years or longer. The reason that law was made was because they thought if a mermaid or merman left their underwater home for ten years and didn't come back, they were trying to expose all merfolk for money. They thought I was a changeling who hadn't come back in ten years. I explained to them that I had never even seen a mermaid or merman before. They and the rest of the merfolk freaked out. How did a human get in, and how did a human have a changeling locket? So now, everyone thinks that I am here to expose them. They call my coming here The Accident."

So that's The Accident! I thought to myself.

"Narayan is my bodyguard now because other merfolk threatened me, and the royal family doesn't trust me. They have him swim everywhere with me to make sure I don't do or plot anything evil."

My jaw dropped. This was a lot to soak in, and this whole time, the royal family was against modeling because they believed Sheila, a model, threatened their lives!

"So, why do you still come here if everyone hates you and you have an amazing life in the human world?"

"I want to know how I got this changeling locket. Out of

all my family members, the person I remember the most is my older sister, Clara. Clara Meela. I came down here to see if she could be alive. I remember her as a human, not a mermaid. But I've checked for her in the human world, and there is no data found on a Clara Meela. So, I'm assuming she's a changeling. She's my only chance of having a family . . . I don't remember anybody else."

"How will you recognize her? It's been so long since you've seen her."

"All I remember are her big, emerald eyes."

"Hmm," I pondered. "I can help you find your sister."

"Really?" Sheila beamed.

"And I have an idea of who can help us—she feels like an outcast in Aquaria, too. Do you know Sharika?"

"Who?"

"Sharika Shark," I said.

"I've never heard of her." Sheila pondered. "Let's go meet her! I've met most of the mermaids in Aquaria, and none of them have been my sister. If she's not my sister, maybe she can at least help us!"

As we were swimming toward the town square, I realized that today wasn't one of the special Sundays where the Changeling Entrance was open. "Sheila, how exactly did you get into Aquaria today? It's not Sunday."

"I have special privileges," she replied. "Since the royal family is just as curious as I am to how I got in, I'm allowed to come back whenever I want to try and solve the mystery.

As long as Narayan is with me, I can come and go as I please."

"That makes sense."

As we swam into the Coral Café, Aqua and Delfina were ordering coffees.

"Hey, Paradise! Hi, Sheila!" Delfina exclaimed.

"I'm so sorry, I don't think we have met before," Sheila said.

"Sheila, these are my friends: Aqua and Delfina. These are two mermaids you can fully trust."

Sheila smiled. "It is very comforting to know that there are some mermaids who will befriend me."

Aqua smiled. "Don't worry, we're not scared of you or Paradise."

"And, you probably don't remember, but we met a couple years ago! You were examining us to see if we were your sister, remember?" Delfina asked.

"Oh! My apologies. I've met so many mermaids that I just cannot keep track!" Sheila exclaimed.

"Excuse me, ladies," Narayan intervened. "But I just got a call from the palace. The royal family would like to see you two immediately." He looked at me and Sheila.

I frowned. "Aqua, Delfina, could you guys do me a favor and look for Sharika?"

"Ugh, why?" Delfina asked.

"Sheila and I would like to speak to her when we come back."

"As you wish," Aqua sighed. She swam out of the café with

Delfina. Sheila and I followed Narayan to the palace.

CHAPTER 11

Do I Know You?

Narayan, Sheila, and I swam through the crystal palace and found the entire royal family sitting in the throne room.

"So, you two are together," was the first thing King William said.

Sheila and I remained quiet.

"The search parties haven't found your locket, Paradise," Queen Christiana said sternly.

"But, Your Highness—" I started.

"I suggest you keep quiet, Paradise," Princess Torrie said.

"You two humans are together," King William repeated. "Would you like to tell us what you are plotting?! Or do you want us to—"

"Dad!" Tatiana stepped in.

"Your Highness, we are not plotting anything!" Sheila exclaimed. "Ask Narayan. He is always with me."

"But Narayan doesn't know what you are plotting while you're in the human world," King William continued. "All of a sudden, this Paradise Jones shows up, and a couple days later, so does Sheila? You are obviously not loyal, Sheila, and you have let in some random teenage girl. Paradise? Is that even her name? Or is she an imposter?"

Imposter? What did he even mean? "Now you have brought her down here for another pair of eyes to help expose our kind. You shall pay the consequences . . . tonight!"

"What?" we both shrieked.

"Your Highness, I promise I came in with a locket!" I cried.

"Then how did you steal it?" King William demanded. "How did you know about—"

"Enough!" Tatiana screamed. The king and queen looked at her angrily. "Please, Mom and Dad. Give her a chance. I trust her."

"Well, I do not!" Princess Torrie stepped in.

"We will come to a compromise," Queen Christiana said. "By tomorrow night, if your locket is not found, we will know you were lying. Something horrible will happen to you two."

I gulped and Sheila looked horrified. Was Sharika right? Was the royal family really out to kill me?

"But I am still trying to find my older sister—" Sheila started.

"No!" King William's voice echoed. "We have already searched for this Clara Meela, but she does not exist."

"You have until tomorrow, Paradise Jones," Queen Christiana said as Sheila and I swam out.

We swam back to the town square in silence. I had until tomorrow night to find my locket. If not, something horrible would happen to me and Sheila.

"Sheila, I'm so sorry you got dragged into this," I said sadly. "I will help you find your sister before tomorrow."

She smiled back. "And I will help you find your locket."

When we arrived in the town square, Aqua and Delfina were waiting for us by the statue of the royal family.

"Well? Any luck in finding Sharika?" I asked.

"No, we haven't seen her all day," Delfina replied. "She really is a mysterious mermaid."

"Well, we must find her before tomorrow night." I filled Aqua and Delfina in on everything that happened. They were shocked.

"To lighten up the mood, do you want to come over for a sleepover?" Delfina asked us.

"I need to get back up to the human world," Sheila said. "I'm paying for a hotel room, and I have an important call to discuss my next photoshoot."

"Me too. I need to gather all of my swimsuits before I leave my family forever," I said. Everyone looked confused. "It's a long story."

"Yeah, I can't come, either. I have a lot of studying to do, considering we've been missing school to help out Paradise," Aqua said.

"It's okay. See you all tomorrow!" Delfina replied. We all waved bye and went our separate ways.

"Paradise, you want to know something crazy?" Sheila asked as we were driving back to the hotel.

"What is it?"

"When I first saw you in the airport, I thought you were Queen Christiana . . . that is, until you took off your glasses."

"Yes, I remember that you thought I was someone else. I was so confused."

"I still think you two look very similar." She paused. "Paradise, what if Queen Christiana is your mother?"

"What?!" I exclaimed.

"How else would you have a changeling locket? How else would you have hair that looks just like the royals?"

"Sheila, many merfolk have brown hair. Plus, my eyes aren't ice blue, remember? It's the sign of the royal family. My eyes are brown."

Sheila slumped back into her seat. "You're right."

"Ladies, we've arrived back at the Sirena Mare Hotel," the driver suddenly said.

Sheila smiled. "You know, Sirena Mare means sea mermaid."

"How was Rome?" I asked my family when I got back to the room.

"Very nice, considering we didn't have to spend extra money on you . . ." Dad said.

"Dad, stop," Sam said.

"Stop what, Sam?" Mom asked. "Your dad is telling the truth. She would've cost us extra money on the trip. And you should only pay for what is worth it."

"That's it!" I yelled. "All my life you have treated me as if I'm not a part of the family. I never understood why until I heard your conversation last night. I'm sorry you were forced to adopt me, and you've been forced to do all of this for me. But you know what? That stops now. I don't need you to do anything for me anymore, because I'm leaving. I'm leaving tomorrow and you will never have to see me ever again!"

Everyone was speechless.

"P-P-Paradise, you don't really mean that, do you?" Mom asked, stuttering.

"The only reason you're asking me this is because you're scared my real parents will come do something horrible to you. And I hope they keep that promise."

"Paradise—wait! Let's come to a compromise . . . " Dad said.

I stormed into my room and slammed the door. I packed

up all of my bikinis and got ready to leave the Jones family for good.

I woke up early the next morning to say goodbye to Sam. He was the only person that I was really going to miss.

"So, you're really leaving?" he asked sadly.

"Yeah, I am. Thanks for being the best big brother I could've asked for." I gave him a big hug.

"Thanks for being a great little sister." He sniffled. "Will you at least come back and visit me?"

"I hope," I said. It depended on if I could find my locket today. Although I was in potential danger going back to Aquaria, I knew the changeling guards would come looking for me if I didn't return, and there was no way I was staying with the Jones family anymore. I had nowhere else to go. In Aquaria, there was still hope.

I grabbed my bag and headed out the door. Sheila and I met by her car, and we drove off. I remained silent the entire drive and boat ride. I still wasn't sure where I was going to live; the royal family probably wouldn't want me staying in Aquaria. Sheila and I quietly dove down to the Changeling Entrance in the Blue Grotto. She opened it with her locket, and we swam in. Millie, Queenie, and Delfina were waiting for us.

"Oh! How did you guys know we were coming this early?"

I asked, startled.

"Queenie and I had a feeling," Millie said.

"And we had a feeling that you'd need to talk to Delfina, so we brought her with us," Queenie said. "See you later."

"Wait—you're leaving now? We could really use your help!" I exclaimed.

"We're going to look for your locket in the outskirts of the city," Millie said.

I sighed in relief. "Thank you."

Millie and Queenie swam off.

"Where's Aqua?" I asked Delfina.

"I'm actually not sure," Delfina pondered aloud. "But I did see Sharika."

"Where?"

"She was by the Deep Crevice the last time I saw her," Delfina replied.

"Well, what are we waiting for? Let's go!" I exclaimed.

"You two go on. I'm going to find Aqua," Delfina said.

"Oh, Delfina, before you go, can you take my swimsuits to your house?" I had been holding on to a bag with all of my bikinis in it.

"Of course!" Delfina said. She took the bag of swimsuits from my hands.

Sheila and I waved and then began swimming toward the Deep Crevice.

"Where's Narayan?" I asked her as we were approaching it.

"He doesn't wake up this early," Sheila said. "I never come here this early. But, since the guard stationed at the Changeling Entrance saw us, he probably called Narayan to come watch me."

"Oh—oh! Sharika!" I exclaimed, spotting her a way's off. Sheila and I quickly swam over to where she was lingering above the Deep Crevice. I looked down the dark crack in the ground. I shuddered. "Sharika, I want you to meet Sheila Meela."

"I know Sheila," Sharika said with her back turned to us. "I don't think we've met. I'm from the Shark family. My name is Sharika."

"Sharika . . . is Shark your married name?" Sheila asked.

Sharika's back was still turned to us. Sheila looked at me hopefully.

"Sharika, do you mind turning around? Sheila wants to know if you're . . . her sister," I said.

Sharika turned around. Her eyes were ruby red.

"Oh . . . Paradise, this is not my sister," Sheila said.

"I do not have a sister," Sharika said.

"Sharika, why are your eyes—"

"Sheila!" A voice cut me off. We all turned around to see Narayan in the distance.

"Oh, my bodyguard is here. Excuse me, I'll be back in a moment." Sheila swam off.

I turned back to Sharika. "Sharika, why are your eyes red? I thought your natural eyes were gree—"

Suddenly, Sharika grabbed my arm and started swimming down into the Deep Crevice.

"Sharika! Sharika, what are you doing? There's a monster that lives down here!" I screamed loudly.

Unfortunately, we were so far down that no one would have been able to hear me. As we kept getting lower and lower, the temperature got cooler, and the Crevice got darker. I thought I saw something move along the walls, but it was too dark to tell. I buzzed with fear. When we got to the bottom, my eyes must have adjusted to the lack of light. I could see that there were shelves of potions of many different colors. It was dark and chilly, and there was a big cauldron in the middle of all the shelves. Suddenly, someone swam out from behind one of the shelves.

"Aqua?!" I exclaimed. "Sharika, we all need to get back to the top before the monster comes and has us for breakfast!"

Sharika rolled her eyes. "Paradise, I *am* the monster."

"WHAT?!" I screamed. "Don't worry, Aqua, we can get out of here!"

Sharika sighed. "I thought you were smarter than this."

"You're here on purpose . . . aren't you?" I asked Aqua nervously.

Aqua smiled. "Yes, Paradise, I'm here on purpose."

"All those nights. They weren't spent studying—they were spent here," I said, connecting the dots.

"Aqua is helping me," Sharika said.

"Helping you with what?" I asked slowly.

"Helping me overthrow the Royales!"

My heart stopped. "Wait a second, did you just say . . . "

"Yes, Paradise, you heard me correctly." Sharika smiled wickedly. "We are preparing to overthrow the Royales."

"The royal family . . . that's *my* family?" I asked in shock. How would I be able to prove it to them? I didn't have a tail and I didn't have blue eyes. There was only one way for me to prove it, but at this point, it was impossible. "I can only prove it with . . ."

"Your locket?" Sharika smirked. "This old thing?" She was spinning my necklace around her finger.

"You've had it this whole time?" I asked.

"It floated all the way down here just last night. I think the current has been pushing it all the way down here since the day you arrived. I found it and knew it was the missing key that could help us take over Aquaria!" Sharika laughed.

"But if I'm a Royale, how come the king and queen didn't recognize me? I know my eyes aren't blue, but I look like Queen Christiana. I'm their *daughter*."

"The first day when you arrived, I cast a spell on you so that the king and queen couldn't recognize you, and you had nothing to prove that you're their blood. I was coming out of the Deep Crevice when I saw Millie and Queenie trying to keep you hidden, and that's when I cast the spell. I immediately knew you were the king and queen's daughter."

"So that's why my body tingled when I was swimming to the secret sand passageways and when I first met you. Your spell!" I exclaimed. "But even without my locket, you knew it was me? No one else has recognized me!"

"Yes, I knew it was you," Sharika said. Her red eyes gleamed. "You're like the human version of Queen Christiana."

"How are your eyes red?" I asked.

"Do you even know how powerful she is?" Aqua laughed. "She changed her eye color to red. If she wants, she could change yours to any color, too."

Then it hit me. The red coal Princess Torrie was talking about must have been a test sample Sharika was doing that accidentally floated up from her lair. The red ring around her eyes was because she was practicing changing her eye color.

"How do you have this much power? Only the royal family—"

"Oh, sweetie, it takes practice." Sharika laughed.

"Aqua, how could you do this?" I asked sadly. "I trusted you."

"Sharika showed me that I was destined to be a part of this! How come Aquaria has the name Aqua in it? Fate must be telling me that this city is meant for me, too," Aqua said. "So, I'm going to help her. I've always just been an ordinary mermaid, but Sharika has shown me my destiny. This is our kingdom now."

Suddenly, bubbles started rising from the cauldron.

"It's time." Sharika's eyes glowed. Aqua grabbed me and tied both of my hands behind my back. I tried to resist, but she was too strong. "First, the blood of those who wish to overthrow. Then, the blood of one who shall be overthrown." Sharika pricked her and Aqua's fingers with an urchin's spine and put a drop of each of their blood in the cauldron. Then, they pricked my finger. I yelped in pain.

"Next, evidence of one of the most difficult spells to master: color changing." She threw in a piece of red coal. "Third, a hair of one killed." She threw in a strand of someone's hair.

"Whose hair is that?!" I asked.

"My husband's." Sharika smiled.

"You killed your husband?!"

"Shark was a fool. He stood in my way. He had the opportunity to help me, but he refused. But he has helped me along the years," Sharika said.

"How did he help you if he was dead?" I asked, shocked.

"SHH!" Aqua screeched.

"And finally, something magical belonging to a Royale." Sharika smiled evilly. She hung the locket in my face, then threw it into the boiling pot.

"NO! My evidence!" I screamed. How was I supposed to prove that I was their daughter now?

After the brew stopped bubbling, Sharika and Aqua cupped the liquid in their hands. Then, they drank it. Their eyes started swirling, and their fingers started shaking. They closed their eyes, and when they opened them again, they were back to their natural color.

"Now we are in our truest, most powerful form." Sharika laughed. She thrust her palm out toward a rock, and it exploded. Aqua did the same.

"No! You can't do this! Not to my only family . . . " I started.

"*We* could have been your family! I told you to work with me, and we all could've ruled Aquaria together. But you chose not to listen. And this is what you get," Sharika said.

"When you said the royal family would kill me, you were lying, weren't you?" I asked angrily.

"Of course. They're not evil. The worst they would do to you is stick you into one of their deepest, darkest dungeons and never let you out."

"What about in the Coral Café when you told me that whole story about your past?"

"Fake," she sang. "Humans truly are so gullible."

"Well, we still have some time until we need to go back up," Aqua said. "Should we go get your summoning horn?"

"Summoning horn?" I asked.

Sharika smiled wickedly. "It's to call all my pets that live down here, just in case we need backup."

"I'll bring Paradise with us so she doesn't escape." Aqua grabbed my shoulder and we followed Sharika into a tunnel behind her shelf of potions.

CHAPTER 12

The Lairs Down Under

As Aqua dragged me through the dark tunnel, I kept hitting the sharp cave walls. It was pitch black and cold, but I could feel that the tunnel was narrow. It smelled smoky. *Impossible,* I thought. *We're under water.*

"Where are you taking me?" I asked nervously.

"Since you're back here with us, we're giving you a tour," Sharika said. "Welcome to my bedroom."

There was a hole in the cave wall that we swam into. Inside was a small bedroom with nothing but one bed and a light.

"Aqua, where do you sleep?" I asked.

"I live with my parents," she said.

"Do they know that this is where you come at night?"

"Of course not," she laughed. "I'm the smartest Marine. They'll never catch me."

We swam out of the hole and continued through the

tunnel. After a minute, we stopped at another hole. When we swam in, there was a desk with many papers and pencils.

"This is my thinking room. I plot everything in here." Sharika smiled deviously.

Under some papers, I saw an old-looking picture of a family.

"Is that your family?" I asked.

"Never mind that!" she screeched and scattered papers over it.

We swam out of the hole and kept going through the tunnel. The next room we went to was the creepiest one of all. It featured about fifteen statues of merfolk with closed eyes and open mouths.

"What are those?" I asked, shuddering.

"Many merfolk have ventured down into the Deep Crevice to find the monster that lives down here. Anytime someone came, I would kill them." Sharika laughed. My mouth dropped open in horror. "I made them into statues so I can always remember my accomplishments. They're my trophies."

"You're sick!" I exclaimed. Sharika snorted. "So, the times you were up in the town square, how did you know when someone came down here?"

"We have security, obviously," Aqua said.

"Security? What kind of security?"

Sharika smiled. "That brings us to our next room."

This time, the hole was blocked by a door with a tiny

window. I peered through. There were sharks, swordfish, stingrays, jellyfish, and octopuses. I nearly fainted in fear.

"You keep the deadliest sea animals in the Deep Crevice?!" I screamed.

"They're my pets. I've put a spell on them to protect the Deep Crevice. When Aqua and I aren't here, the swordfish hide along the walls of the Crevice. They hide below twenty feet, and if anyone comes lower than that, the swordfish will attack. If the mermaid or merman somehow passes the swordfish and swim deeper, there are transparent jellyfish. If the sting of the jellyfish doesn't hurt them, and they reach the bottom, where my shelves of potions and cauldron are, there are camouflaged sting rays hiding in the sand. If somehow they pass those, and see that there's a tunnel behind one of my shelves of potions, and enter it, there are sharks that roam the tunnels. And finally, for extra protection, I have an octopus guarding each room entrance."

I shook with fear. "Why do you need all that protection?"

Sharika smiled. "Welcome to the final room." We swam into the last hole in the cave wall. Inside was a big laboratory. "In here is where I create my potions. I have a book of spells handed down to me from . . . well that doesn't matter. I make my potions and bottle them up. I store them outside the tunnels by my cauldron which we threw your changeling necklace into—as you saw. Pretty cool, right?"

"No! Not cool at all!" I said.

Sharika just laughed.

"Sharika, we need to go," Aqua said. "It's almost time that the royal family will be looking to throw Paradise and Sheila in the dungeons."

Sharika smiled. She took her summoning horn, grabbed me by the arm, and started swimming out of the tunnel. Aqua followed us as we swam up and out of the Deep Crevice. My heart was racing. I didn't know what was to come.

CHAPTER 13

Paradise Royale

Sharika and Aqua dragged me to the town square. Everyone was crowded around the royal family.

"Has anyone seen Paradise Jones?" King William said to the crowd with a glare. "Sheila Meela won't tell us."

"I promise I don't know where she is!" Sheila said in tears.

All of the merfolk shrugged their shoulders and were looking around in fear.

"She's here," Sharika said as she and Aqua dragged me toward the family.

"Well, do you have your locket?" King William asked.

"It's all her fault!" I cried angrily, looking at Sharika.

"Do not blame other merfolk for your lies!" Princess Torrie said.

"Hand her to us, please," Queen Christiana said. Sharika and Aqua smiled at each other and let me go.

"Thank you for finding her. How can we repay you?" King

William asked.

"Give me your kingdom," Sharika said.

"What?" Queen Christiana asked.

"Give me your kingdom, or fight us."

"Who are you?" Tatiana demanded.

Sharika smirked and swam so that she was above all of the merfolk. "My name is Clara."

"From what family?" Tatiana asked slowly.

Sharika looked right into Sheila's eyes. "The Meela family."

Sharika Shark is Clara Meela?!

"Clara?!" Sheila cried.

"Are you . . ." Princess Torrie started.

"The sister Sheila told you about? Yes, that's me," Clara said.

"Wh-why did you never tell me?" Sheila trembled. "I've been looking for you all these years!"

"Because you're the reason our parents died!" Clara said angrily. "It's all your fault!"

The merfolk gasped.

"But how?" Sheila cried.

"Many years ago, our parents came from another ocean kingdom where magic was allowed. When they moved to Aquaria, the king of that time, King William's father, told them that only the royal family was allowed to use magic in Aquaria. Our parents were forced to close down their magic business, and they became very poor.

They decided to move to the Deep Crevice because they didn't have enough money to pay for a house. When you and I were born, they saw how exceptionally beautiful we were. And then they realized we were changelings. Our parents wanted to give us an opportunity to become highly paid models and not have to suffer such harsh lives as they did. They sent you to the human world when you were five just in case I failed down here as a model. When we dropped you off with a new family, I secretly gave you a changeling necklace. Our parents didn't want to give it to you, so that you could live a normal human life, but I wanted to be able to reunite with my little sister again one day. Obviously, it took you more than ten years to figure out what it was, which is why you cannot turn into a mermaid."

The town square was silent; the merfolk were listening intently.

"On our way back to the Changeling Entrance after dropping you off with your new family," she continued, "we got into a car accident. I was the only one who survived. I was upset and angry; it was all your fault. We were on our way back from dropping you off. When I got back to Aquaria, I was the only one living in the Deep Crevice.

Since then, I've been practicing magic none of you could ever dream of. When I heard about The Accident, I got married and changed my last name to Shark. I changed my first name to Sharika. I didn't want to meet you because it was your fault our parents died."

"Clara!" Sheila sobbed. "Clara, it wasn't my fault. I'm sorry! I'm so, so sorry."

"Why do you want to take over our palace?" Penelope asked, clutching Tatiana's hand.

"To restore our riches in honor of my family. The Royales are the reason my parents had to shut down and suffer! And now it's your turn!"

"You can't fight us alone," Queen Christiana said. "You're not powerful enough."

"Maybe not just me, but I have Aqua Marine to help," Clara said. "I realized her intelligence and strength and am using her to help me overthrow all of you."

"Aqua?" Delfina asked, surprised. "But why?"

"Aquaria has my name in it!" Aqua shouted. "That means there is something in this for me. I've always been treated as an ordinary mermaid, but this could put my intelligence to good use!"

"That's why you're helping this witch?" Princess Torrie exclaimed.

"Aquaria's name has been here for thousands of years! You have nothing to do with it, you foolish girl!" Queen Christiana said.

"Blah blah blah blah blah," Clara said. "Aqua, let's take what is ours!"

They thrust their palms toward the royal family's statue, and it exploded. The merfolk screamed, swimming in all directions. Clara and Aqua started blowing up shops and freezing the merfolk's tails.

Millie and Queenie quickly swam up to me. "Paradise, there is not much time. We can take down Aqua, but you must be the one to take down Clara," Millie said.

"Did you know this whole time that I'm a Royale?"

"No, not until Clara threw your locket into the cauldron. We had this feeling that we needed to go back home. When we got there, we saw in our crystal ball what had happened." Queenie said. "We couldn't make it in time to tell the royal family, though."

"Do they know I'm a Royale?"

"No—" Millie started. Suddenly, a ball of fire came rushing toward our heads. *Fire under water?!* We quickly ducked. "Go, Paradise—hurry!"

I quickly started swimming toward the royal family.

"There is only one way to stop evil magic like this." Queen Christiana nodded. She held her hand out and said, "Christiana Royale."

"William Royale," King William said and held her hand.

"Torrie Royale." Princess Torrie reached for her dad's hand.

"Tatiana Royale." She clutched Princess Torrie's hand.

"Penelope Royale." Penelope grabbed Tatiana's hand.

"Alexander Royale." Prince Alexander held Penelope's hand.

Although I thought this was very dramatic, I swam up next to Prince Alexander. "Paradise Royale." The entire family looked up at me. I held his hand. Suddenly, I felt a pop in my eyes. I turned toward King William and Queen Christiana.

King William's jaw dropped. "Your eyes . . . they're blue."

"Who cares?!" Clara yelled. As she thrust her palm toward me, Queen Christiana broke free from our family chain.

"That's my daughter!" she yelled. She opened her hands wide and made a pushing motion toward Clara. All of the family's combined power struck Clara's body. The strike was so strong that it cracked her tail and summoning horn.

"How dare you!" she screamed. Suddenly, she made a huge ball of fire. "This is for ruining my life, and my tail!"

She threw the fireball at the royal family. At *my* family.

"No!" I shouted. After all these years, I had finally found my family. I wasn't about to lose them again.

I swam in front of them and held my hand out. Suddenly, a ball of blue light came shooting out of my palm. Her fireball and my ball of blue light clashed and then exploded. Suddenly, Clara turned into a statue. As I looked down at myself, I saw my legs disappearing and a mermaid tail forming! All of the merfolk looked at me in shock.

"Paradise!" I heard Queenie call. I turned around. Millie and Queenie were both holding Aqua by each arm. "What should we do with her?"

Delfina immediately swam by my side. "This is for being a liar!" Delfina smacked Aqua on her cheek with her tail.

"And this is for trying to overthrow my family." I smacked

Aqua's other cheek with my new tail. I felt so strong having a tail!

"Owww!" she whined in pain.

"Now, what should we do with you?" I asked. "My family is very powerful. We could freeze your tail, or even better, break your tail. Or, we could turn you into a statue and place you and Clara with the rest of her *trophies*."

"Violence is never the key," Princess Torrie said, swimming over to me. "Oh, my goodness—she's under a spell!"

"What? What do you mean?" Delfina asked.

"Her eyes . . . her pupils are shaped like octagons!" Princess Torrie said.

"How were you able to see that?" I asked in shock.

"Remember, I strive to know every inch and detail about Aquaria and its magic," Princess Torrie said. "I pay very close attention to things." She put her thumbs on Aqua's closed eyes and said a spell. When Aqua opened her eyes, she started crying.

"Your Highnesses, I am so, so sorry! Clara put me under a spell years ago, and I wasn't able to break it. It made me evil!" Aqua cried.

Delfina rushed over and gave Aqua a big hug. I sighed in relief. I was glad Delfina wasn't about to lose her best friend.

I suddenly felt a hand on my shoulder, and I turned around. "We have a lot of explaining to do," Queen Christiana said.

CHAPTER 14

The Curse

King William invited all of Aquaria to the palace for an overdue explanation. The merfolk gathered in the throne room as my family and I swam to the front. I was still getting used to my new tail, but it was so cool!

"Kingdom of Aquaria," King William announced. "I know you all have many questions for us. We would like to start off by saying that we are sorry for hiding the truth of Paradise from you. We just thought it would be best for our safety."

"Sixteen years ago, I gave birth to my middle child, Paradise," Queen Christiana said. "We were thrilled she would have two big sisters and hoped she would have younger siblings, too. The night before Paradise was born, the palace chef told us he had heard of a new, healthy soup that would be good for the new baby. After I drank it, I grew very ill.

Millie and Queenie Reef's parents came and examined my soup. They said it had been cursed!

"We immediately fired the palace chef and asked the Reefs what would happen to Paradise. They said she would never be able to grow a tail and that there was no remedy to counteract it. Without a tail, Paradise could have been harmed easily. Our tails are very magical, strong, and they keep us protected."

"We decided to take Paradise to the human world where she could lead a better life without harm," King William continued. "We dropped her off at one of the best orphanages in France. We didn't keep her in Italy because it was too risky. If a changeling saw her, they would immediately be able to recognize the resemblance between Paradise and our family."

"When we dropped her off at the orphanage," Queen Christiana continued, "we gave her a changeling locket so that she'd have something from us. Once William had walked out of the orphanage, heartbroken, I decided to change Paradise's eyes to brown—just in case she ever ran into a changeling. They would be able to recognize her blue eyes immediately."

"After seven years," King William said, "we found out that she still hadn't been adopted and that a new lady had taken over the orphanage and made the girls live in horrible conditions. We didn't want our daughter to live in misery, so we used the Changeling Entrance for the second time. We went back to France and looked for a nice, happy-looking family.

That's when we saw the Jones family. The parents seemed so loving and got their son whatever he wanted. We approached them and asked if they would adopt Paradise; if they said no, we would look for another family. We offered them gold, and they said yes. We told them if they took our gold, but didn't adopt Paradise, we would do something horrible to them."

"So, they adopted Paradise," Queen Christiana continued. "When Paradise first found Aquaria, we thought she was an imposter who had somehow found out about our daughter and was trying to be her so that she could become royal or overthrow us. Initially, we thought she could be our daughter, but then she said she hated her family. We thought the Joneses were good people. And she didn't have her locket as proof that she was our daughter, so we didn't know what to believe. We had her spend time with our children to see if they liked her, and they did."

"You also didn't know it was me because Sharik—I mean, Clara—cast a spell so you couldn't recognize me," I said.

"But how did we know nothing about Paradise?" Princess Torrie asked.

"We erased everybody's memory of her once we realized she was cursed," King William said sadly. "We didn't want merfolk to know she was in the human world. It would be a greater risk, and if there were merfolk who didn't like us, they could have gone and harmed her."

I was speechless. "Then how did Clara recognize me?"

"When we erased everybody's memory, we set the magic spell all throughout the city of Aquaria. We didn't send the curse to go underground, which is where Clara was apparently secretly living . . . in the Deep Crevice."

"Was it really the chef who cursed Paradise?" Tatiana asked.

"After hearing Clara's story, I don't think so. It must have been Sheila and Clara's parents who recommended the curse-filled soup to the chef. They were the only merfolk in Aquaria who knew how to use magic before William's father banished it. They were probably angry, which is why they cursed me!" Queen Christiana said.

"I can't believe this," I said.

"Are you mad at us, Paradise? We tried to do what was best for you," Queen Christiana said, teary-eyed.

I thought for a while. "No. You tried to do what was best for me, even though it turned out bad. I left the Jones family for good, so now I can be with you!"

My siblings gave me a big hug while the surrounding crowd clapped; I could tell that they forgave their king and queen.

"Now we know that Aquaria is safe," Queen Christiana said. "The statue of Clara will be moved to a heavily guarded place."

"And we need to clear out the Deep Crevice!" Aqua exclaimed from the crowd. "There are some horrible things down there."

"And we need to apologize to Sheila," I said. "She has never meant any harm, and now we know for sure that she is a changeling."

The crowd nodded their heads in approval.

"Can we grow her a tail?" Penelope asked.

"That magic is too strong, even for us. If we could do that, we would have given Paradise a tail ages ago," Queen Christiana said.

"That's okay!" Sheila exclaimed. "Having the merfolk's approval of me is more than enough!"

The royal family smiled.

"I just have one question: how did I grow this tail?" I asked.

"The curse probably lifted when you defeated someone related to the curser," Millie said. "That must be the remedy!"

"All hail Princess Paradise!" Prince Alexander cut in.

"All hail!" The crowd responded.

I beamed. I had never been so happy in my life. I was finally with my family, in a magical underwater world, and a princess. I couldn't ask for anything more!

"I'm so happy I can live with you all forever!" I cried and hugged my parents.

They both embraced me. "We are, too."

CHAPTER 15

Still an American Girl

After everyone left the palace, my family, friends, and I had a grand dinner, set up in honor of me coming home. I was *home*. We insisted on the Reefs, Dolphins, Marines, and Sheila joining us. Torrie (yes, I didn't have to call her Princess anymore!) was shocked and a little upset that she knew nothing of my birth, but she eventually loosened up and understood it was for all of our own safety. She, Tatiana, Penelope, and Alexander seemed overjoyed to have me as their new sister.

"I am so excited that you're living here now!" Delfina said. "Now we can have sleepovers every night!"

"And I can finally come!" Aqua cheered.

"And we won't need to escort you all the way to the Changeling Entrance every day because you'll be here!" Queenie cheered. Millie gave her a look. "What? It's far from here!"

"Actually," *Dad* cleared his throat. "Christiana and I were thinking of sending Paradise back to the human world."

"What?" we all exclaimed.

"You haven't finished your education!" *Mom* said. "We also tapped into your transcript and took a look at it; Aquaria's technology is advanced, so we were able to see your grades."

"So you basically hacked into my school account?" I asked.

"That's not the point," Mom said quickly. "Your grades aren't good. You don't want to be known as 'the failing princess who dropped out of high school.'"

"But what about spending time together? And where will I go?" I asked.

"As much as we are longing to spend time with you, we can't be selfish. This is the best thing for you. Plus, it will give us time to make you a beautiful room," Mom said.

"Who will I stay with?"

"Didn't you say you were popular?" Aqua asked.

"I guess . . ."

"Would your best friend be willing to let you stay with her?" Delfina asked.

"She's offered before. She knows how Paul and Megan treated me. I never stayed with her, though. Her family already pays so much for her sister's medical school and Zahara going to Charm High. I didn't want them to have another kid to worry about."

"Well, since she's offered for you to stay with her many

times, I think you should give her a call," Sheila said.

"And we can send money with you to help them with the extra costs," Dad added.

As much as I didn't want to leave Aquaria, my family was right. Getting my education was important, and I was finally realizing that. I couldn't help rule a kingdom and be a slacker!

"Jayla Henderson," I said into my shell phone. It started ringing.

"Paradise?" Jayla answered.

"Hi, Jayla. I have to ask you something."

"Your voice sounds really strange . . ."

"International calls, I bet," I said. "Anyways, I called to ask if I could live with your family until high school is over. I know it's an abrupt question and a lot to think about, but just hear me out. I finally met my true parents. They live here in Italy! But we decided that I should finish my education at Charm High. I won't be going back with the Jones family, and I know Zahara keeps telling me to come live with your family. I know since you're at university there's a bedroom open and my real parents said they'd help with the extra cost of me living with your family . . . "

"Of course!" Jayla said. "Paradise, I am so proud that you're coming to finish school. You can definitely stay with us. One question, though, why didn't you just ask Zahara?"

"I want to surprise her!" I exclaimed. "But first, I need to ask your parents. I wanted to make sure it was okay with you first if I took your room."

Jayla laughed. "You're on speaker, and when you brought up living with us, my parents both nodded their heads. Don't worry, though, Zahara is in the hotel lobby buying snacks. She doesn't know a thing."

"Good," I said. "See you soon."

I smiled brightly. Looks like I would be living with Zahara for the next two years!

After we ate our delicious dinner, Aqua and I had a sleepover at Delfina's. We talked about all the adventures we'd had in the past week; it's crazy how your life can change so quickly. Over the next few days, I spent all my time with my family. I played blocks with Alexander, had tea parties with Penelope, raced with Tatiana, and helped Torrie solve more of her mysteries.

As spring break started coming to an end, it was time for me to go back to Los Angeles. Everyone was teary-eyed as I left. I was gifted a new changeling locket so that I would be able to come back every break and summer before I graduated. Because it was a very long swim, I decided to fly back home. My family couldn't fly with me because it was dangerous for them to risk their lives in the human world. They couldn't risk getting into a car crash or catching an unknown sickness. Sheila was kind enough to fly back with me, even though she had just gotten back home to Italy.

My mom also put a spell to change my eyes back to brown whenever I went to the human world. It would be very odd if I went back to Los Angeles with blue eyes!

When we landed in California, Sheila took me shopping for new clothes. I had left everything in my hotel room, and I had forgotten my bikinis at Delfina's house. After our shopping spree, Sheila drove me to Zahara's house. I hadn't seen or spoken to her in two weeks, and I couldn't wait to surprise her.

I knocked on the door anxiously. Zahara opened it.

"Paradise?" she asked, surprised.

"Zahara!" I exclaimed and gave her a big hug.

"You haven't spoken to me in weeks!" she said.

"That's because—you won't believe it—I met my real parents and siblings!"

"They were in Italy?"

"Yes! I dropped the Jones family for good!"

"Finally! You have to tell me everything."

I smiled, knowing I couldn't do that. I only told her I found my family at the Amalfi Coast when I heard their last name. I couldn't expose the merfolk or Aquaria, even though she was my best friend.

"Where are you staying now?" she asked.

"Well, I was hoping I could stay with you."

"Yes! You can, bestie!" she hugged me again. "So, if you aren't with the Joneses anymore, who drove you here?"

I smiled. "Sheila Meela!"

"What?!" she screamed. Sheila waved from the car and Zahara nearly fainted.

"So, Zahara, my parents and I decided that I would finish high school here and then go back to Italy and live with them. So, I have to ask you something. Would you like to be my study buddy for the next two years?"

"Actually study? And get good grades? No more caring about popularity?" Zahara asked. I nodded. "Okay! Jayla has been pressing me for a while about doing well in school, and I could feel myself about to crack. Everyone treats her with so much respect because she's smart. People don't treat us nicely because of our brain; they treat us nicely because of our beauty!"

"Exactly! So, are you in for aiming for straight As?" I asked.

"I'm in!"

I had a new motivation. I wanted to do well for my family, friends, and my new kingdom. There was no stopping Paradise Royale now!

BACK TO THE PRESENT: JUNE, END OF TENTH GRADE

I am now in English class, finishing my transformation essay for Ms. Art. After spring break, I apologized to all of my teachers and told them I promised to do better. Since my grades were in the C and D range, I wasn't able to bring all of them up to As by the end of the year. My teachers told me I ended with high Bs and low As, which is still a huge improvement for me.

Today, Ms. Art asks me and Zahara to stay after class. She reads our essays and grades them in front of us. After a few minutes, she looks up with a huge smile on her face.

"Ladies, you have finally done it. You have finally received an A on a paper, and an A in my class!"

Zahara and I cheer and hug each other. Ms. Art is beaming, and we give her a hug, too. Zahara and I proudly walk out of the classroom. We know we have accomplished something big this year.

❧ CHAPTER 16 ❧

Graduation

I am now back in Aquaria with my family. I'm twenty-eight years old . . . I know, crazy. I just settled here a month ago and am ready to live here forever. You're probably wondering why it took me ten years to move back after graduation. No, it didn't take me that long to graduate high school. So much has happened since sophomore year, but I'll backtrack to the days after finishing tenth grade.

After not seeing the Jones family for a couple months, I had cooled down. I hadn't spoken to them since I left. Sam tried getting a hold of me; I told him I was fine. We were on two different sides of the campus at school, which kept me from seeing him.

His graduation was the day after my last day of tenth grade. Because he had always supported me, I decided I should go to support him. Zahara asked if I wanted her to accompany me, but I told her it was better if I handled the

Jones family on my own.

When I arrived at the graduation, I sat alone. It was emotional to see Sam in a cap and gown. He had committed to New York University. I knew he would make a great film director one day. As the ceremony was going on, I recognized two familiar faces: Paul and Megan. I took a deep breath and walked over to them. I decided to be mature and to forgive them. I didn't want them living with the idea that I could be out in the world anywhere. Even if they were cruel to me, I knew a part of them wanted to make sure I was okay.

"Hi," I said. They both turned around, shocked.

"Paradise?" Paul asked.

"Yup, it's me."

"How—how did you get back? Where did you go?" Megan asked.

"I found my real family in Italy. That's who I have been with," I said.

"You found them," Paul repeated my words. "They were so selfish!"

"No, Paul, you guys were selfish," I said. "You didn't care for me like a real daughter. But I'm here to say that I forgive you. You don't need to live the rest of your life thinking that you broke me. I am stronger than ever now."

They sat there quietly for a moment. "I remember your parents offered us a lot of gold to adopt you. Are they still rich?" Megan asked.

I laughed. They had no idea. "Yes, very."

Megan gritted her teeth. "Since we have taken care of you for so long, can we get some more gold?"

Was she out of her mind? "Sorry, but no. Shouldn't my forgiveness be enough for you guys to live a satisfied life? You don't need to worry about me anymore, and I've forgiven you. Is that not enough?"

Megan started breathing heavily and looked like she was about to explode. "Why do you get all the special privileges? Why do you deserve any of this? I'm the one who had to deal with you; I deserve this!"

"Megan, breathe," Paul said. "But, you're right. Paradise doesn't understand how much love we gave her."

I didn't know what to say. They were still the same heartless people. I decided to be mature and just walk away. After the ceremony, Sam was thrilled to see me. I gave him a big hug and congratulated him on his success. I told him I was happy and got better grades in school, and he was very proud. We said goodbye, and I promised to visit him in New York.

SENIOR YEAR

Zahara and I were finishing our final college essay in her room. It was an essay on something that transformed us from the beginning of high school to now. Many people told me that I shouldn't have applied to the top colleges in the world because my grades were poor for ninth grade and the majority of tenth grade. I didn't listen to them, though.

I wrote about how I used to be a slacking student until I met my real family. They transformed how I felt about school and gave me a new drive for learning. I ended my junior year with straight As. I also talked about how I joined the swim team. It was the beginning of senior year, I was already acing my way through, and I was one of the best swimmers on the team.

"Done!" Zahara exclaimed. She was applying for a degree in biology; she wanted to work alongside Jayla. I, on the other hand, was interested in business.

You're probably wondering why I was even applying to college. The deal with my family was to graduate high school and come back to Aquaria forever. That *was* the plan, until I had a dream during the beginning of junior year. It was a dream of a promise I had made many years ago. Even though I made that promise when I was seven, I still remembered it as a seventeen-year-old.

That's when I told my parents I wanted to go to college. They wanted me to come home; they said to use Aquaria's riches to fulfill my promise. I refused. It was Aquaria's money, not mine. Plus, Aquaria needs its money to make the city thrive. If I took their money, I would be taking away millions of dollars that should be used to help the mermaid world. It would make Aquaria poor, which is not what I wanted. I told my parents that I would go to college, get the best job I could, make my own money, and then go fulfill my promise.

TWELFTH GRADE GRADUATION

It was graduation; the day had finally come. Even though I told my parents not to risk their lives by coming to the human world, they still came to congratulate me. Zahara and I excitedly did our makeup and put on our cap and gown before the graduation.

After the ceremony, I gave her a big hug. "Zahara, we did it. We finished high school."

"And we got into amazing universities! I still can't believe I got into UCLA. Two years ago, I would have never imagined this!" she squealed.

I wouldn't have, either. I chose to go to Cambridge University, one of the best colleges in England. I would have stayed in America, but England was closer to Italy, and I wanted to be near my family.

"Zahara, I'm going to miss you so much." I sniffled. "Thank you for everything."

She started crying. "I'm going to miss you too! Promise you'll come and visit me every year?"

"I promise."

Tatiana and the rest of my family came racing over to me. "Paradise—you did it!"

"I'm really proud of you, Paradise." Torrie smiled.

Penelope and Alexander were holding a bouquet of flowers for me, and my parents gave me a big hug.

"Oh my gosh. Are these your parents?" Zahara asked excitedly.

"Yup! Meet my family," I said brightly.

As Zahara mingled with my parents and siblings, her family approached us. I gave them all big hugs.

"Thank you for taking care of me. You don't know how much I appreciate you all," I said to them.

"We love you, Paradise!" Zahara's mom said.

"And we love you," Mom said, turning to Zahara's parents. Our parents struck up a conversation while Zahara and I said goodbye to the rest of our friends.

Suddenly, I felt a tap on my shoulder. It was Ms. Art.

"Paradise. Zahara. I am so proud that you ladies got into amazing universities. I will miss you both so much!"

"Thank you for teaching us such valuable lessons, Ms. Art. We will miss you, too!" I said. Zahara and I each gave her a hug.

We finished saying all of our goodbyes and then went to dinner at my favorite restaurant: California Pizza Kitchen. Afterward, we took a flight back to Italy. I wanted to get to Aquaria as soon as possible so that I could see Aqua and Delfina's graduation.

Even though I had horrible jet lag, we made it to the graduation in time. It was a surprise that I was coming, and they were thrilled to see me there. The school gave us the grandest seats to sit in; each of us sat in our own big clam with cushions and pillows. We sat on a balcony above all the merfolk and graduates; it was amazing! I loved being a princess.

After their graduation, we went to the Rainbowfish Restaurant. It was my first time going, and the restaurant was beautiful. It was bright with colors, and there was a show starring many rainbowfish. We ended the night toasting with the merfolk's number-one treat: the mermaid milkshake. I wish we had it in the human world; it was the most delicious dessert I have ever tasted! It was a strawberry milkshake with whipped cream and just a pinch of mermaid sprinkles.

I stayed in Aquaria for the entire summer and had the best summer of my life. It was hard to leave when it was time to go to Cambridge. My family reluctantly let me go after we swam to England. I was sad and also scared; I had never visited Cambridgeshire—or England, for that matter. It was time for a new journey; but by now, I was used to going on adventures.

CHAPTER 17

Retracing My Steps

Cambridge University was like a castle. It had beautiful stonework with grand archways and was near grassy fields and a beautiful river. Sometimes I wished to hop into the river and swim to Aquaria. Unfortunately, the river didn't spill out into the ocean.

I studied most of the time in college. I didn't want to get too close with anyone because I knew after I set up my business and made money, I would go back to Aquaria and never see anyone from Cambridge again. I kept my circle of friends small. My closest friend was my roommate, Ashlyn. We would study together and visit London on long weekends.

London was a beautiful city; I loved the chimneys on the houses and the double-decker buses. Whenever we went to London, we took strolls in Hyde Park, a huge, green, peaceful park with lakes and ponds. We would go to the seven-floor mall, Harrods, and shop for the entire day. At night, we would watch plays and dine in London's top restaurants.

When we weren't studying or in London, Ashlyn would go to parties. As much as I wanted to go, I knew I had to be safe. The human world is much more dangerous than the ocean. I would spend those nights studying even more, but I knew it would pay off. Eventually, I was the top student of my class. I was very proud of myself for coming this far.

On holidays, Ashlyn would go back to her home in Ireland, and I would take the Changeling Entrance in the city of Somerset back to Aquaria. The Wookey Hole Caves were my way in and out of England. Even if it wasn't the Sunday of the month that the entrance was open to changelings, my locket would always activate and let me in. The swim to Aquaria was about four hours. It wasn't as bad as if I went to school in America, but my parents would always send a mermaid taxi for me. The mermaid taxis are large clam shells with cushions and pillows (like the ones we sat in for the graduation at Seahorse High School) pulled by a whale. On the times I would visit Aquaria as a surprise, I would swim two hours, spend the night in Sealandia, and continue my journey to Aquaria the next day.

Three years after I graduated from Cambridge, I opened up a fashion and makeup company. I was shocked at how successful my company became. I still had a love and passion for fashion and makeup, and that helped me create it. Being stationed in Milan, Italy, had me much closer to the Changeling Entrance on the island of Capri. I even asked Sheila to model for my clothes and makeup line—which she gladly accepted. After my company became worth many millions of dollars three years after I created it, I sold it, and knew it was time to put my money to good use.

I took a flight out to Paris a week after I had sold my company. I asked Zahara to come because I hadn't seen her in a while. We spent a few days visiting the Eiffel Tower, fancy chateaus, art museums, and cafés. The last time I had been in Paris was twenty-one years ago with the Jones family. This time, I didn't have to hear Megan and Paul complain about wasting their money on me in the hotel. Now, I stayed in a beautiful hotel with pride; I had gotten myself there with all my hard work.

After we spent some time in Paris, I took a train by myself to Pauvres-Kalai. I hadn't seen or heard from Rosie since I left Ophelia's Orphanage. I didn't know if she or the other girls would still be in Pauvres-Kalai, or if they would be somewhere else in the world.

When I arrived, the town was exactly the same as I had left it. Nothing had changed . . . nothing except for me. I was coming back with new memories, new intentions, and a new family. As I passed by beggars on the street, I gave them all money and left them with a warm smile. When I finally arrived at the orphanage, I stood in front of it; nothing had changed, besides the sign. Now it just read: *Orphanage*. I took a deep breath and knocked on the door. I heard someone quickly shuffle down the stairs.

"Bonjour," a little girl said, opening the door.

"Hi, may I come in?" I asked. She nodded and opened the door. It was the same as I had left it. Creaky, narrow stairs, a room at the top of the stairs, an eating room at the bottom, a small bedroom, and a bathroom. "Is Ophelia still here?"

"Non," the girl said, confused.

"Who takes care of you?" I asked.

"Mademoiselle Rosie."

"Lannea, who are you speaking to?" a voice said, coming from the back room. It was Rosie. She was all grown-up. She had her hair pulled back into a bun and was wearing a simple dress. "Bonjour. How may I help you?"

I smiled. "Rosie, you don't remember me?"

"I have never met an American before," she said.

I took out my locket from under my shirt and showed it to her. Her eyes grew wide. "Paradise? Paradise Royale?"

"It's me, Rosie!" I said.

"Oh my goodness!" she said and gave me a big hug. "Where have you been all these years?"

"Los Angeles, the Amalfi Coast, Cambridgeshire, and Milan!"

"Wow! You have seen so many places!" she exclaimed. "I haven't left Pauvres-Kalai once."

"You run the orphanage now?" I asked.

"Yes, I do."

"What happened to Ophelia?"

"Ugh, Ophelia." She gagged. "She got fed up with us

when I was about twenty. She took all the money from the orphanage and moved into a small cottage in the countryside by herself. So, I took over the orphanage. I didn't want to, but I knew it was the right thing to do. I couldn't just leave these young girls uncared for!

"All of the girls older than me left for jobs and are working in small shops throughout Pauvres-Kalai. You are the only one who has become rich—which I am assuming by your travels and clothes."

"And I'm here to share that with all of you." I smiled. "I want to donate all of my money to make your lives better—the orphanage and the rest of Pauvres-Kalai. I have five-hundred million dollars to give."

"Five-hundred million?!" Rosie exclaimed. "Paradise, are you crazy?"

I just laughed. After I gave away all my money, I'd go back to being the princess of Aquaria. I wouldn't need my money down there.

"I'm serious. I want to make this orphanage a beautiful home for children. I'll add a pool, playground, kitchen—you name it."

"Oh, Paradise!" Rosie started to cry.

"And I want to find a new owner for the orphanage. You've been here all your life. You should get out, find a job, or get married!" She hugged me again and wept some more. "And I want you to tell me where the rest of the girls work. I want to give them money, too."

After Rosie cried some more, I gave her my money and went to look for the other girls throughout Pauvres-Kalai. They were all overjoyed to see me and receive their money. I told them not to take it all for themselves, but to make Pauvres-Kalai a more beautiful place, and they listened. I promised to come back and visit to see the transformation of the poor city into something beautiful. By far, this was my favorite part of my vacation in France.

CHAPTER 18

Sea Sweet Sea

After my trip to France, I moved back to Aquaria for good. Torrie is now thirty-three and queen of Aquaria. Mom and Dad still live in the palace and are delighted that their eldest daughter is doing an amazing job ruling the kingdom. Her knowledge of Aquaria has made it a better and safer place. All of the merfolk love her. She is getting married next year to the king of Sealandia, but they will live in Aquaria's palace while ruling over both kingdoms.

Tatiana is now thirty. She has opened up her own after-school sports club. She coaches the young and teen merfolk in all of her favorite sports. They go to tournaments throughout the different oceans. Penelope is seventeen and a junior in high school. She gave away all of her stuffed animals to the younger kids of Aquaria and Sealandia. Although, she did keep her tea set. We all have a tea party once a week with her. Alexander is fifteen and just starting high school. He's definitely a ladies' man; he has so many mermaids chasing after him!

Millie and Queenie are all grown up now, too. They are twenty-three years old and work in the palace. They are still the smartest mermaids in Aquaria and always work alongside us if there is any trouble. Aqua and Delfina now lead groups of mermaids and mermen in adventures around the ocean. They venture to the deepest depths of the ocean and to the highest points they can reach.

Mom and Dad finally mastered the most difficult spell of all: changing merfolk into changelings. They don't just grant that power to anyone because it's a risk to our kind, but they've granted it to Aqua and Delfina. The two of them take adventures to different places in the human world. We've taken vacations together in Hawaii, Greece, the Bahamas, and Bora Bora, so far. They are obsessed with traveling and are fascinated by the human world.

Zahara and Jayla are now two of the top doctors in America. They take trips around the world and cure sick patients. Zahara and I keep in touch a couple times a week, and she still thinks that I'm living above water on the Amalfi Coast. Even though Sheila is thirty-two, she is still one of the top models of the human world, but now also of the ocean. Merfolk don't give her dirty looks anymore, and she's made many friends. As for Sharika, or Clara, as we now call her, she's been locked up as a statue for twelve years. The guards cleared out her potions and animals in the Deep Crevice and have opened it up for tourists.

You're probably wondering what happened to the Jones family. Sam became a big-time movie director. He only offered to give his parents some of his money if they apologized to me. Although it was a forced apology, I was thankful for the call.

Finally, me. I help Torrie rule, but I also opened up fashion and makeup stores all throughout the ocean. The merfolk love the stores, and I decided to fulfill my dream from a long time ago: becoming a model! I only model for my clothes and makeup in the ocean, though. I now spend most of my time having fun with my friends and family down under.

About the Author

Tara Lala lives in Los Angeles, California. She has enjoyed writing for fun since she was five years old. Her other hobbies include playing basketball, doing martial arts, and playing the piano. She began writing *Tails from Down Under* when she was fifteen years old, and it is inspired by all of her favorite travel destinations in Europe. Her favorite vacation spots are Capri, London, Santorini, and Lake Como. You can check out her other book, *Twincesses*, and follow her on Instagram @taralalaofficial for more!